字在飛邊

李鎮成的文字藝術

Borderless Calligraphy:
Chen-Cheng Lee's Series of Script Art

目次
Contests

館序

　　李鎮成先生一直從事文字藝術之研究，其作品豐富而多元，極具原創性，深獲國內外藝壇肯定，被視爲現代文字藝術創作的原生型典範之一。「悉曇系列」與「千字文系列」是他近年繼文字皴系列之後的最新力作。前者係以悉曇字爲主體，運用篆刻及雕刻的造型表現，結合天然石材的質感與悉曇字的線條張力，表達一種生命內在的冥想與觀照。後者則以中國古代書家研習最久最廣的千字文爲創作對象，由千字文的豐富組合及變化中表現漢字的多義特質，進而探尋中國書法所賦予現代文字藝術創作最大限度的審美價值。

　　李先生的文字藝術系列創作，源自他對傳統書法藝術與文字意涵之體會，但他並不滿足於只是繼承或充實傳統的元素。他一直勇於以現代的造型觀念去詮釋漢字的特性及書法藝術的豐富內涵。從創作歷程言，其文字皴系列可視爲其對傳統的轉換，而悉曇文與千字文系列則是此種轉換之擴大與延伸。經由這些歷程，使得李鎮成的文字藝術系列創作具備某些時代意義，而不只是古典藝術的翻版，也不是傳統的任意變形；它是一種有生命的再生與創造。

　　藝術最可貴者爲提供人類共同心靈永恆流動之憑藉。它可以是傳統的延續與發揚，也可以是全然的創造；然無論如何，其詮釋總以作品、創作者，及觀者所處的時代爲核心。國立歷史博物館長期以來即重視傳統及現代藝術轉換之研究與創作鼓勵，藝術家本人長期專心致力於文字藝術創作，其系列作品有一定的時代性，故本館樂於介紹與社會大眾。

國立歷史博物館館長

 謹識

2008年5月

Preface of National Museum of History

Chen-Cheng Lee has dedicated his life to calligraphy (the "art of the written word"). The body of works that he has produced over the years is both immense and varied, displaying enormous creativity, and the quality of Lee's calligraphy is widely recognized in art circles both in Taiwan and overseas. He is generally considered to have been one of key figures in the development of contemporary word art in Taiwan. The "Siddham" and "Thousand-character Essay" series represent his most recent masterpieces, following on from the "Calligraghy Tsuen" series. The "Siddham" series is based on the Siddham script that was traditionally used for writing Buddhist scriptures in Sanskrit. Lee has applied the techniques of seal-carving and engraving to this script, combining the textures of natural stone materials with the powerful linear structure of Siddham to express both deep meditation and concern for others. The "Thousand-character Essay" takes as its subject matter the thousand-character essay form that was the focus of so much study by the Chinese calligraphers of antiquity. By leveraging the complex structure and variation that characterize the thousand-character essay, Lee is able to bring across the multiple levels of meaning that Chinese characters embody, exploiting to the utmost the aesthetic values with which traditional Chinese calligraphy endows contemporary word art.

Lee's script art series have their roots in his study of traditional calligraphy and the meaning of writing. Not content merely to follow tradition, Lee has consistently sought to use modern concepts of form to interpret the unique features of Chinese characters and to explore the deeper significance of calligraphy. The "Calligraghy Tsue" series could be said to mark the point at which Lee began to transform the tradition; the "Siddham" and "Thousand-character Essay" series represent a continuation of this process. Through these series, Chen-Cheng Lee has made Chinese script art relevant to the modern age, rather than allowing it to degenerate into a rehashing of an ancient art form. At the same time, Lee's work does not treat the tradition casually; rather, it constitutes a rebirth or recreation of the vitality of traditional calligraphy.

The most valuable feature of art is the way that it provides a vehicle for the eternal flow of the spiritual aspects of human nature that are common to all humanity. Art can be an extension or enhancement of tradition, or it can make a clean break with tradition to create something totally new and innovative. Either way, the core element in the interpretation of work of art is the era in which the work, the artist and the viewer have their existence. Over the years, the National Museum of History has undertaken extensive research on the process of transformation from traditional to contemporary art, and has sought to encourage the creation of art in this field. Chen-Cheng Lee has dedicated many years of his life to word art, and the various series of works that he has produced have great significance for the times in which we live; the National Museum of History is delighted to have this opportunity to present some of Mr. Lee's latest works to the general public.

Huang Yung-Chuan
Director
National Museum of History

字在無邊——李鎮成的文字藝術

　　李鎮成是一位充滿創作生命力的藝術家，他的藝術成果早在二十餘年前就已揚名於1980年「東京都美術館書法展」、1987年「第二十八屆中日親善書畫展」。尤其近十餘年來，鎮成先生創作更加旺盛，幾乎年年有展覽活動，長年經營，累積了豐碩的成果，更在藝術界擁有一片天地。

　　李鎮成2006年的「文字皺」系列書法作品，令人耳目一新，且具有內涵深刻的意象之美。書法是非常具有民族特色的一種藝術，不但在生活中具備表達、交流思想的實用功能，更可提升為獨立的線條藝術。

　　從李鎮成先生歷年的作品看來，他特別熱衷於以「石」為載體，以「文字」為表現元素，藉由此兩種形式傳達自己的藝術理念。他認為石頭是具體而微的山水縮影，彷彿自然生成的，因此在他眼中，每塊石頭都和崇山一樣，他的心情是尊敬仰望的。

　　以鑿刀結合畫筆，以金粉結合水墨，以書法結合繪畫，更結合雕刻。李鎮成從平面的「文字皺」走向立體的「文字皺」，他藉形式開發內涵，馭古典跨越現代，開拓出更遼闊的藝術新境。

大葉大學董事長

謹識

Borderless Calligraphy:
Chen-Cheng Lee's Script Art

Chen-Cheng Lee is an artist full of creative vitality and his artistic achievements were already well known since the "Calligraphy Exhibition" in Tokyo Metropolitan Art Museum in 1980 and "The 28th Taiwan-Japan Calligraphy and Painting Exhibition" in 1987. In the past ten years or so in particular, Mr. Chen-cheng has shown more creative drive and staged exhibitions almost annually, his long-term efforts give a high yield and he can hold his own in the artistic circle.

Chen-Cheng Lee's "Calligraphy-Tsuen" series in 2006 are refreshing and meaningful in terms of conveying the beauty of imagery in calligraphy. Calligraphy is a unique Chinese art, it is not only functional in expressing and exchanging thoughts in daily lives but can be enhanced as an independent linear art.

Looking at Chen-Cheng Lee's works in the past years, he is especially keen on using "stone" as a medium and "character" as an element of expression to convey his artistic concepts through the two forms. He regards a stone as a miniature of landscape, it is almost naturally formed and in his eyes every stone is like a mountain, which he respects and admires.

Combining a chisel with a calligraphy brush, combining gold powders with ink, and combining calligraphy with paining and even sculpture, Chen-Cheng Lee marches from the one-dimensional "Calligraphy-Tsuen" to the three-dimensional "Calligraphy Tsuen". He gives meanings to calligraphy lines and dots, commands the classical art while crossing over to modern art to expand into a wider new vision.

Hwang, Jeng Shyong

Hwang, Jeng Shyong
Chairman
Dayeh University

無邊界的創作——讀李鎮成文字藝術系列

蘇啟明　藝術史博士

　　李鎮成一直從事文字藝術，其作品豐富而多元，極具原創性，深獲國內外藝壇肯定，被視為現代文字藝術創作的原生型典範之一。「悉曇系列」是他近年繼文字皴系列之後的最新力作，其創作元素係以悉曇字為主體，運用篆刻及雕刻的造型表現，結合天然石材的質感與悉曇字的線條張力，表達一種生命內在的冥想與觀照。而千字文系列則以中國古代書家研習最久最廣的千字文為創作對象，由千字文的豐富組合及變化中表現漢字的多義特質，進而探尋中國書法所賦予現代文字藝術創作最大限度的審美價值。

虔誠與尊敬－李鎮成的悉曇系列

　　所謂悉曇字（Siddham）是一種流行於北印度的古代梵語書寫文字，它產生於公元第五至第六世紀。據研究，古代印度很早便有文字，其中較有系統的為盧文（Kharosthi）和婆羅迷文（Brahmi）兩種，悉曇字即由後者演變而來。它是一種表音文字，有五十一個字母，南北朝末期便傳入中國，隋唐時代佛教興盛，梵文是當時中國最流行的外國語言之一，而當時所稱的梵文實際即悉曇文字；所謂的梵文佛教經典便多以這種文字寫成。後來隨著密宗佛教興起，悉曇一詞更被泛指一切與佛教修行有關的學問。

　　古代印度婆羅門教認為聲音是一種神靈，極為重視。密宗佛教繼承婆羅門教這一傳統，也認為聲音有不可思議的力量，而表示聲音的符號也因此具有種種神祕的功能，於是在密宗佛教所使用的悉曇字中便發展出各種代表佛或菩薩的「種子字」，且進而依其形、音、義衍生出諸多不同的觀行法門。由於對聲音的崇拜，必然重視祈禱時的讚頌和咒語，這些讚頌及咒語的文句甚至文字本身便是神聖並具有法力的，密宗稱為「陀羅尼」，漢譯為「真言密咒」。

　　悉曇字後來在印度隨著佛教的沒落與蒙古人入侵而漸漸不再被使用，在中國也逐漸為蒙古文和西藏文所取代；但在日本則因密宗佛教的流行而一直使用到今天。密教也是在唐代傳入日本，其關鍵人物為空海，他於公元九世紀初來到中國，遍訪各地高僧，後拜在當時密宗大師惠果門下，盡學金剛界與胎藏界兩派密法，同時也學會悉曇文字，是日本歷史上第一個掌握梵文的學者。空海在中國時更廣泛結交中國文士，曾隨韓方明學習書法，揉合顏真卿與王羲之兩家之長而有所創造，在日本被視為書聖；他留存迄今的墨跡有〈風信帖〉及部分悉曇字帖殘片，筆勢雄渾，神韻躍動，不僅是日本書法正宗，也是後來所有悉曇書法流派的祖源。日本使用悉曇字除了宗教因素外，最重要的還因為日本人把悉曇字當作一種藝術來學習和欣賞；而隨著時代環境演變，悉曇字的藝術性且逐漸勝過宗教性。

日本原來的悉曇學研究也以音韻爲重心，到江戶時代才轉而研究悉曇的語意，進而發展出帶有審美意義的悉曇書法，並分爲澄禪、淨嚴、慈雲三派。因悉曇文字本爲表音文字，其字形結構與表意或象形的漢字極爲不同，但受到密教的影響，其書寫非常嚴謹及講究；也因此使其書法能在藝術上有所發揮。根據目前日本悉曇書法主流慈雲流的傳習心得，認爲悉曇書法的精神首在於「神」，其次在「勢」，再次爲「力」。爲了使每一個悉曇字都具備這三種條件，書寫者必須熟悉每個字母的筆順，但爲了追求寫出來的藝術效果，各家筆順有時又會有所不同，因此就形成了日本悉曇書法的各個流派。如慈雲流便以流暢見長，而淨嚴流則以雄健爲特點。除了漢字以外，世界上再沒有一種文字像悉曇字這樣被賦予如此豐富而多采的藝術審美精神。然而也正是由於日本人發展出來這套悉曇書法審美價值與系統，才使悉曇書法能超越宗教與語言的界線，成爲人類共同的重要藝術文化資產。

　　李鎮成本來便有深厚的書法素養，其長期投入的文字藝術創作也一直以漢字爲元素。無論是漢字的字型、字義乃至字音，他不僅都曾作過許多藝術性的轉換，甚且加以有意識的解構與還原以探討漢字的藝術性本質。基本上李鎮成對文字是非常敏感的─特別對文字內在的藝術質素有一種異乎尋常人的敏銳度。悉曇字之所以吸引他首先便是其文字本身婉轉多姿的藝術性；其宗教性反而是次要的。不過，與他過去用漢字作爲創作元素的歷程相同，李鎮成發現悉曇字之所以美，似乎不全由於字的外在形體；就和漢字一樣，形、音、義三者是不能分割的，創作者與欣賞者也不可能完全分離，少了其中一項就構成不了其藝術性。悉曇字也是如此，如果將其被賦予了千餘年的宗教意義抽離掉，那樣的悉曇字是沒有生命的；而沒有生命的悉曇字自然也不會具有任何藝術張力！

　　李鎮成一直是以全副的生命及他對生命的嚴肅態度從事藝術創作。他創作的文字藝術尤其多一分虔誠與尊敬。他在「悉曇系列」中精進學習，其作品予人們一種無限的祥和及寧靜感；正如「悉曇」一詞的本義，是一種互證的圓滿，也是一種自證的成就。

傳承與發揚─李鎮成的千字文系列

　　千字文據傳是公元六世紀初梁武帝命員外散騎侍郎周興嗣依殷鐵石所模王羲之書跡一千字不重複者編綴而成；據說周興嗣一天便完成了，原名爲《次韻王羲之書千字》，後世簡稱爲《千字文》。又有另一種說法是三國魏太守鍾繇所書，而王羲之再加以改寫者。後者開頭幾句爲「二儀日月，雲露嚴霜，夫貞婦順，君明臣良」；前者起首爲「天地玄黃，宇宙洪荒，日月盈昃，辰宿列張」幾句，即現在通行的版本。

　　歷代書家以千字文爲書寫對象者極多，因此留下的千字文書跡不少。其中較有名者如隋智永〈眞草千字文冊〉、宋徽宗〈草書千字文〉卷、明張弼〈千字文〉卷等都是名跡。智永的〈眞草千字文冊〉以正楷和草書二體並寫，歷來評價極高，影響亦極深遠，如宋代米芾便稱譽曰：「智永臨集千文，秀潤圓勁，八面具備。」清代梁巘則說：「書法自右軍後當推智永第一，觀其〈眞草千字文〉圓勁秀拔，神韻渾然，已得右軍十之八九，所去者正幾希焉。」宋徽宗的〈草書千字文〉則呈現另一種神韻與風格,其書體為狂草,一氣呵成,筆勢凌空:變幻莫測,猶如大江奔騰,一瀉千里,運筆迅疾流暢,而結體奇宕瀟灑,極為書家珍視。張弼的〈千字文〉卷也是草書,亦帶有狂草筆意,頗富個人色彩。民國以來則以于右任的〈標準草書千字文〉最有名,其運筆自然流暢,字字清晰而錯落有致,體勢雄健有力,可學可玩,極富開創性,是近代珍貴的文化資產。

歷代書法家之重視千字文並屢為傳寫者,主要是因為這一千個單字幾乎涵蓋了最常用的漢字之半,而在漢文字的發展歷程上,這些字基本都已定型;更重要的是其造型結體係根據王羲之的書法而來,具備各種審美元素,故不僅是學習認字的啓蒙教材,也是研習書法乃至從事書道創作的不竭泉源。據說智永生平便寫了各體千字文八百通分送江南各寺院,作為有志學書者的範本,可見以千字文為書法研習或創作指南自始即是中國書法界有意識的發明,也是所有從事書道藝術創作者必修的傳統藝程。

面對如此人人熟悉的千字文書法,今人如要別開生面的據以創作並不容易。然而李鎮成在經過長期從事文字藝術創作的歷程後,卻覺得這一千個漢字仍充滿著時代的生命力。第一、千字文本身就是一篇很好的文章,其內容包羅萬象,且充滿耐人尋味的雋永名言。第二、千字文四字一組、兩組一句的排比方式,高度而精簡的將漢字的辭意予以活化,很多詞句根本就成了常用的成語,如「寒來暑往」、「秋收冬藏」、「弔民伐罪」、「空谷傳聲」、「寸陰是競」、「夫唱婦隨」、「同氣連枝」等不勝枚舉。追本朔源,千字文原來並非出自同一篇文章,而是從許多文章和字跡中編綴成的,但連綴出來的千字文卻產生了嶄新的意義,而這些新的意義又反過來融入到各個時代中,成為人們普遍的思想意識。就此而言,其文化意義自是遠遠超過文字本身所能賦予的範疇了。

通過對千字文的歷史及文化研究,李鎮成的千字文系列自然而然要用一種新面貌呈現。他把這一千個字分別刻為一千個造型單元,每個造型單元皆由一個字組成(其實就是一個字)。這一千個造型單元可以任意組合,一個、兩個、三個、四個、五個,乃至百個、千個等。而每一種組合都可以產生不同的意義;若不加以組合,則每一個單元本身就是一個字,它的意義也是多重的。這裡透露著漢字最關緊要的一個特質,即每個漢字本身都是多義的;把幾個漢字組合在一起便產生許多不同的詞意或句意。李鎮成將每個造型單元裡的字分別呈現在相鄰的立體平面上,此與他從前的文字皴系列中總是反覆用不同的字體刻同一個字於一件作品上,有異曲同工之妙,它們都是為了呈現漢字這種一字多義的特質。此種造型構思及手法可謂是一種獨創,而其藝術效果也非常成功。

流傳一千五百餘年的千字文,對李鎮成而言不僅是其從事文字藝術作的養分,更可以視為其文字藝術創作的突破口。他以一種前所未見的造型方式精確的表現了漢字的形、音、義多重而富變化的特質。

轉換與創造

藝術最可貴者為提供人類共同心靈永恆流動之憑藉。就藝術的表現意涵而言,它可以是傳統的延續與發揚,也可以是全然的創造。然無論如何,其詮釋總以能具時代意義為起碼要件;藝術的原創性在此,傳統的再生性也在此。藉著些富有創造性的意涵，不同地區、不同族群，乃至不同時代的人們，心心相映，相互感會，這正是藝術的價值。

　　李鎮成的文字藝術系列創作，源自他對傳統書法藝術與文字意涵之體會，但他並不滿足於只是繼承或充實傳統的元素。他一直勇於以現代的造型觀念去詮釋漢字的特性及書法藝術的豐富內涵。從形式層面言，他的文字皺系列是對傳統的轉換，而悉疊文系列則是此種轉換之擴大與延伸。就漢字的特性言，其豐富多重的詞義性無疑是最難用語文以外其他方式表達者。而李鎮成的千字文系列則用一種化整爲零又可多元組合的造型單元，成功的表達這種特性。因此從內容上看，千字文系列是一種創造。

　　正是有了這種創造，才使得李鎮成的文字藝術系列創作具備時代的意義，他絕不是古典藝術的翻版，也不是傳統的任意變形；它是一種有生命的再生與創造，是我們可以留給後世的東西。

Borderless Calligraphy :
Chen-Cheng Lee's Series of Script Art

By Chih-Ming Su, phD in History

Chen-Cheng Lee has been working on script art for more than three decades. His works are abundant and diversified with originality which is affirmed not only in Taiwan but also in the international art industry. He is regarded as one of the originators of contemporary script art. The "Siddham" series is his latest work followed by "Calligraphy Tsuen". The major achievement of his creative work is Siddham, which expresses inward observation and review of life by the nature of stone and tension. His series of "Thousands Character Classic" is created from study of the original "Thousands Character Classic", the oldest and most extensive collection of classic characters which are studied by all ancient Chinese calligraphers. Expressing the polysemous of Chinese characters by understanding the plentiful combinations and variations, we can proceed to explore the maximum aesthetic beauty of calligraphy.

Sanctity and respect:
Chen-Cheng Lee's Series of Siddham

Siddham is an ancient Sanskrit of North India generated in the 5th and 6th centuries A.D. According to research, ancient India has script going back before the development of Siddham. There were two scripts more systematic: Kharosthi and Brahmi. Siddham was developed from the latter one. It is a script performed via pronunciation with 51 characters. It spread to China during the late Southern and Northern Dynasties (420-589 AD). While Buddhism bloomed in the Sui Dynasty and the Tang Dynasty, Sanskrit was one of the most popular foreign languages at that time. Siddham actually is the Sanskrit used in that period of time and most Buddhist scriptures were written in this script. Followed by the springing up of Vajrayana (Tantric Buddhism), Siddham had become a knowledge related to the study of Buddhism.

Brahmanism of ancient India thought that the sound of the script were types of gods and attached importance to them. Vajrayana accedes the traditional belief that the sounds of Brahmanism have incredible power. Therefore, the symbols of sounds also possess a variety of mysterious functions. Thus, Siddham developed the "Hri" (the seed character) to present Buddha or Bodhisattva, and then derived many different initial approaches of observation from the forms, sounds and meanings of scripts. Due to the worship of sound, they respect the praise and charm of praying. All these words and sentences of praise and charm are thought holy and with power in Buddhist doctrines. It is so called "Dharani" in Vajrayana and translated to Chinese as "Mantra".

Followed by the degeneration of Buddhism in India and the invasion of Mongolian, Siddham was no longer used in China but replaced by Mongolian and Tibetan. But in Japan, Vajrayana is still popular and Siddham is still circulated. Vajrayana was pasted into Japan in the Tang Dynasty, the key person for this was Master Kūkai, a Japanese Monk, who visited China in the 9th Century to visit eminent monks, and Master Huiguo initiated him into the esoteric Buddhism tradition, Kūkai was the only one who received the entire teaching of both the Garbhakosha and the Vajradhatu mandalas. Kūkai was also the first scholar who mastered Sanskrit in Japanese history. He widely made friends with many literates in China and learned calligraphy from Fan-Ming Han who mixed Yan Zhengqing and Wang Xizhi's virtues and became the calligraphy Master in Japan. His preserved calligraphy works are "Letter to Saichō" and some remnant copybooks of Siddham. His calligraphy is very forceful with fluent movement. His works are not only the orthodox school of Japanese calligraphy, but also became the fountainhead of Siddham Schools. Except for the religious factor, most importantly, Japanese appreciate and learn Siddham as a study of art. With changes of the times and circumstances, the art of Siddham is gradually exceeding its religious aspects.

The study of Siddham in Japan was focused on phonology, but turned to a study on meaning of the language in the Edo Period, then developing Siddham calligraphy with aesthetic meaning, and was divided into 3 Schools: Zen, Yen, and Yun. Because Siddham characters are originally sound characters, its structure is totally different from Chinese characters which are ideograms and pictographs, but influenced by Vajrayan with very rigorous and exquisite writing which brings into full play its art. According to the current mainstream of Siddham calligraphy in Japan - Yun School - the main spirit of Siddham calligraphy is it's "energy", and "momentum" is the second, and "power" is the last. To make each Siddham character own these 3 spirits, the writer has to be familiar with the order of each stroke, but to achieve the artistic effect, every writer has formed his own way in writing and so doing has formed different Schools. For examples, Yun School is good at fluency, and Yen School is good at energy. Except for Chinese characters, there are no other characters as Siddham characters that own such plentiful artistic spirits. Nevertheless, Japanese developed the aesthetic value and system of Siddham calligraphy to surmount the boundary of religion and language, to make it become an important common artistic cultural asset of mankind.

Chen-Cheng Lee has profound calligraphy capacities and always uses Chinese characters as the elements of his art works. Regardless of the formation, meaning, or pronunciation of Chinese characters, he has not only done some artistic transformation, but also worked on the nature of characters by conscious decomposition or restoration. Basically, Lee is very sensitive to Chinese characters - especially extraordinary sharpness to the inherent artistry and characteristics. The major reason why Siddham attracted him was because of the tactful and variety of the words; the religion is the minor. Nevertheless, as in the same mechanism as Lee's creation by using Chinese characters, he found out the beauty of Siddham not only because of its extrinsic shape, but also because of its formation, meaning, and pronunciation are non-dividable. Moreover, the creator and admirers are non-dividable. Missing any one of them, the art can't be established. That's what all adds up to Siddham. If you separate the religion out of it, Siddham becomes dead and of course without any power of art. And of course, Siddham words without life have no any artistic tension either for sure.

Lee devotes himself in art creation with his life and his serious attitude to life. His creative sun characters are also full with religiousness and respect. He learned depth from the "Siddham" series and showed us a boundlessness peace and harmony. As is the nature of "Siddham", it is a type of satisfaction of mutual-testimony and also an accomplishment of self-testimony.

Heritage and enhancement:
Chen-Cheng Lee's Series of Thousand Character Classic

The original "Thousand Character Classic" said that Emperor Wu of the Liang Dynasty commanded Zhou Xingxi to print and edit the mould of 1,000 unrepeated words of Xizhi Wang's calligraphy in the early sixth century. Reputedly, it was done within one day and the original name was "Secondary Refined Thousand Characters Written by Xizhi Wang", but abbreviated as "Thousand Character Classic" in later age. Another statement is that "Thousand

Character Classic" was written by Mayor Gun Zhong in Wei Country of Three Kingdoms period and was rewritten by Xizhi Wang. The latter version started with "Sun and Moon are two instruments; thin dew and heavy frost; loyal husband with obedient wife; liberal monarch and virtuous people." The former version is the current common edition which begins with "The sky was black and earth yellow; space and time vast, limitless; Sun high or low, moon full or parsed; with stars and lodges spread in place."

Many calligraphers of past dynasties imitated the "Thousand Character Classic"; therefore, a lot of copies have been kept. Some of them are well-known such as the version written in real-cursive-script by Zhi Yong of the Sui Dynasty, written in cursive-script by Emperor Huizong of the Song Dynasty, and the copy written by Zhang Bi in the Ming Dynasty. Zhi Yong's copy was written in both regular script and cursive script which was highly valued and also influential far and deep. Mi Fu of the Song Dynasty commended Zhi Yong "Zhi Yong's "Thousand Character Classic" as smooth and powerful, and well organized." Liang Xien of the Chin Dynasty said, "Zhi Yong is the number one after Yo Jun in the calligraphy field, viewing his "Cursive Script Thousand Character Classic" with powerful and beautiful strokes, natural and harmonious spirit, he is about the same as Yo Jun and few can compete with him." The work of Emperor Huizong of the Song Dynasty presents another style. He wrote in wild cursive script with overwhelming strokes, changing irregularly liking river falling down, fluent and fast writing but with dashing and special structure which was highly valued by calligraphers. Zhang Bi's writing is also written in cursive script with some kinds of wild intention which is a very personal style. After Republic Era, Yu Youren's "Standard Cursive Thousand Character Classic" is the most famous copy due to his natural and smooth strokes, clean and refined arrangement, and powerful figure which owns educational and entertaining value that is very initiative and becoming the precious cultural asset of modern times.

The reason why the calligraphers of all the past dynasties respect the "Thousand Character Classic" and repeatedly imitated it is because these thousand characters contain almost half of the most frequently used Chinese characters, and these characters have completed shaped. More importantly, the structure of words is based on Wang Xizhi's calligraphy which possessed all kinds of aesthetic elements to make it become not only a textbook of recognizing words but also the source of the study of calligraphy and creation. It was said that Zhi Yong wrote 800 copies of the "Thousand Character Classic" in different scripts and distributed them to temples in Southern YangZhi River Area as the model for those people who wanted to learn. It is obvious that the "Thousand Character Classic" is the guidebook for studying or creating calligraphy. It is not only a conscious invention in the Chinese calligraphy field but also a compulsory traditional course for all creators working on calligraphy.

It is quite difficult for current calligraphers to write a refreshing work on such a well-known classic. Through chronic artistic creations on Chinese characters, Lee thinks these thousand Chinese words are still full of contemporary vitality. First of all, "Thousand Character Classic" itself is a wonderful literary work with comprehensive content and intensely interesting and meaningful sentences. Secondary, the arrangement of "Thousand Character Classic" is formed by four words in a set and two sets becoming a sentence. Simple but profoundly activating the meaning of Chinese words. Most terms and sentences are idioms in common use such as: "as summer goes and winter comes", "harvest in fall and store in winter", "relieve the people and right the wrong", "the empty valleys broadly resonate", "an inch of time is to fight for", "the husband leads and the wife accompanies", "united in the blood they share", etc. that are too numerous to enumerate. Trace its source and you will find out that all these terms are not originated from the same articles, but compiled from many articles and handwritings which result in brand-new meanings. These new meanings blend into every era and become people's general ideology. In regards to this, its cultural meaning far exceeds the characters being entrusted.

By studying history and culture in the "Thousand Character Classic", Chen-Cheng Lee's series of "Thousand Character Classic" is of course to be presented in a new outlook. He carves these 1,000 characters into 1,000 modeling units separately and each unit composes only one character. These 1,000 units can do any kind combination randomly with as many as you want, even hundreds or one thousand. Each combination produces different meanings, and even not combining them, each unit is a word itself and its meanings are multiple. Here discloses an important characteristic of Chinese characters which is that every Chinese character itself is multi-meaning. Combining several characters can produce many different terms and sentences. Lee presents each character of each unit on adjacent three-dimensional surfaces. These are different tunes rendered with equal skill as his "Series of Calligraphy Tsuen" for presenting the multiple meanings characteristic of Chinese characters. This modeling conception and technique is so called an original creation and its artistic effects are very successful.

"The Thousand Character Classic" has been spreading for more than 1,500 years. To Lee, it is not only the nutrient to but also the breach of his character art creation. He precisely presents the variety of shapes, sounds, and meanings of Chinese characters with an unprecedented way.

Conversion and creation

The most valuable part of art is to provide human beings an accordance of eternal mutual spiritual interaction. As the performance of art, it could be the lasting or enhancement of traditions, or completely creation. However, the basic condition of art is that the interpretation should be meaningful to the times. The original creation of art is based on this and so is the traditional revival. By these creative meanings, people from different areas, different races, or even different times, they all have mutual affinity and can understand each other - this is exactly the value of art.

李鎮成的悉曇文雕刻作品評析

胡懿勳 上海大學藝術研究院副教授、藝術學博士

前言

　　「悉曇字」（Siddham）(注1) 這個專有名詞，頗為深奧和冷闢地出現在我的眼前，經過李鎮成的解釋，我彷彿有印象曾經在哪些關於佛教的研究中提及，卻從未曾對悉曇字有更深入的認識和探究，對這種文字的陌生，更甚於雲南少數民族的摩挲文字或者西藏文字。李鎮成新進的作品中，以這種北印度的古老文字為主題，創作一系列的與佛法義理和對現世生活祈願有關的雕塑作品，將造型語言提升到視覺之外的音與意的融合。

　　透過李鎮成的引導和介紹，我才能逐漸了解悉曇文字的背景，漸漸進入他現階段創作的主題和創作的理念，並對這類的作品進行一次系統性的觀察與分析。若要深入分析李鎮成這次悉曇字的系列作品，必須聯繫到他前十年以中國文字為母題的創作脈絡中，梳理兩個階段之間是否有所關聯，或者是一個全新的創作階段。而李鎮成中國文字的作品與他自己生活有著密不可分的淵源 (注2)，因此，本文主要從作者論的基礎上，探討李鎮成的創作風格變化和以現階段作品為主的分析。

　　如果耗費過多篇幅擷取悉曇字研究學者的成果，照本宣科地解釋我依然陌生的悉曇文字，反而妨礙對作品的分析與觀察的主要目的，因此，對於悉曇文的歷史、發展和演變等背景，將這方面學有專功的林光明先生著作《簡易學梵字》內容節錄於附錄中，以便於參照背景 (注3)。在作品詮釋與解讀方面，針對悉曇字的特性，有限的文字描述往往容易陷入詞窮的窘境，因此，對造型的分析或多過於悉曇字義解釋，避免臆測成分和盡量不以文害質。

探索新根源

　　乍看之下，一直以藝術創作為職志的李鎮成對悉曇文的興趣似乎有點突兀，他既非文字學的學者，也未曾在文字學領域展露自己的研究成果，更遑論這種北印度古老文字在台灣的學術界也未曾佔據重要地位。表象上看，似乎只是他率性而為的舉動而已。然而，過於簡單的理由，又不能符合李鎮成在創作上確實已經具備創作體系的脈絡，因此，有必要進一步分析他選擇新主題的根源性問題，使我們較能認識他的發現依然源自於與前一個時期創作的一貫理念。

　　僅僅在佛教界，尤其是密宗的佛學研究有些許探討的悉曇字，確實顯得十分艱深和冷闢不可多求。也可以想見李鎮成在尋找相關資料時，必定遭遇許多困難。他訪遍台灣的各大書局和委託朋友在日本尋找悉曇文的書籍和資料，對於他解決悉曇文翻譯為中文意義和悉曇文的書寫等前期的準備工作，提供必要的條

件；這些舉動讓人感受到李鎮成抱持著一股研究的態度，在創作之前付出許多鑽研的心力。畢竟這只是爲創作的準備，他主要的目的是尋找能在創作上發揮的養分和素材，李鎮成的主要用意是從佛教義理出發，悉曇文成爲他探索源頭的一條線索而已。

就生活的背景因素而論，李鎮成學佛多年，禪坐、燃藏香、讀經是生活中的程序，對悉曇文的涉獵也是由於他在尋找佛經書籍與資料的過程，所發現的源頭關聯。無論在生活或者創作，李鎮成有一貫的信念，「尋找源頭」成爲他生命歷程的關鍵詞。在他雲林的老家儲備了各種雕刻用的石材，他對使用過的每一種石材的產地、產量和特性都瞭若指掌；一件作品所需要用的原料，他可以耗費三年時間追索找到原產地，取得自己需要的數量。這樣的精神可以與他選擇「佛陀的文字」——悉曇字，表示創作主題的源頭，作出直接的連接。在他的理念中，梵文的佛教經書典籍和梵唱的佛音根源何在，如何能夠將安靜清淨的音義意象化？他從逐漸以三年時間在悉曇字中找到一些解答。

李鎮成應用悉曇文字中有所謂的「種子字」(注4)，一個字代表法界的佛或菩薩本尊的意涵，將「音」和「意」體現在造形之上。種子字是悉曇字的基本表音符號，卻包含更多的語意在其中，這可能是令李鎮成著迷之處，他在這個源頭裡探究的並不是佛法或者佛學的義理，更多是爲自己解決創作的雕刻語言問題。悉曇字本身的字型極爲簡練，近似符號的悉曇單字，卻又蘊涵大量的佛教訊息，從書寫的表現上，又能如同書法一般的表現線條的曲折柔韌。對李鎮成而言，不啻爲發現一個最純粹的雕刻語彙。

從創作角度而言，李鎮成以中國文字爲主題的創作是有清晰的脈絡可循的，可能這是我們可以將兩種完全不同體系的文字作爲創作主題，唯一能找到的線索；亦即，「文字」形與意的結合，對李鎮成具有相當高的吸引力。李鎮成雖然追究過北印度的悉曇字傳入中國在歷史上發展經歷，然而他更高的興趣卻在於如何將這些比中國篆體字具有更簡練的形，和以音表意的北印古文字轉化在自己的創作之中。

新發現與舊聯繫

從前期的鑽研之後，2005年至2008年正式開始連續的悉曇字的雕刻創作，原本從佛經而來的悉曇字，李鎮成依然保持文字本身的源頭意義未加以重新詮釋，卻更重視這些字形意象的表現。

過去十餘年，他以漢字爲主題的創作，從印面篆刻的形式轉化爲文字的立體空間形式，大致完成兩個階段的創作風格特色，近三年(2005～2008)的悉曇字創作，似乎回歸篆刻式的造形語言，卻與十年前的《道德經》（參見80頁圖）在創作理念上有頗大的差距。他將悉曇字提煉爲極簡的表意符號，卻掌握書寫時具有中國篆字的性質，以書寫形式表現北印古文字的形式美感。這種處理方式掙脫了過去他對中國文字的熟悉的「閱讀與表述」方式，使造型語言純化的程度提高許多，我們會在作品上看到不斷重複的某種符號，形成類近紋樣的圖式，反覆、規律的反覆製造均衡的意象，卻不是讓人能夠閱讀其中的文字意義，或者這些文字表述一個完整的概念：早期的中國文字作品包含這樣的創作意圖，而悉曇字的作品卻屏除了這些複雜的文字閱讀系統。（參見49頁s《大慈大悲咒心咒》6件一組，2006年作，遼東石）

小型長方體系列作品《文殊五字咒》（7件一組）、《百字明》（5件一組）、《大慈大悲咒》（一組29件）等，在保持四方的外觀前提，李鎮成實質上用悉曇字的書法性線條，破壞了四方體積的完整，凹陷的部分襯托出線條的實體，既是平面的游走又有三度空間的轉移，這讓我們不得不需要全方位地觀看這類的作品。觀看李鎮成的咒語作品，就像是藏密轉輪（注5）的意義一般，「從勸世人有發于菩提心者，能推輪藏，是人即與持誦諸經功德無異。」（《神僧傳》卷四）

瀟山石是他擅長使用的石材，李鎮成曾經耗費十年時間在追蹤瀟山石的產地來源，和掌握充足數量支持自己的創作，經過長期的摸索，他自信地掌控媒材所能夠發揮的特性，在悉曇字主題的創作中，他選定瀟山石和遼東石等兩類主要的媒材，自有他充分的理由。瀟山石呈暗紅色，遼東石、青田石則是綠色調有如軟玉的質感。這兩種色調石材著力發揮的不僅是沉穩的體積量感，它們的色彩更能彰顯悉曇字涵意上寬廣度，經過細密打磨的暗紅色瀟山石和細微綠色變化的綠色系石材，帶有透明的視覺感受，削弱石頭的重量感，增強潤澤的柔性質感。

在石材的表面處理方面，他應用日本浮世繪的水溶性顏料，礦物屬性的金粉配合石材的本色，使作品看起來生機盎然。紅色與金色雖然在西藏密宗是主要的色彩，但是，李鎮成沒有特意強調宗教的象徵意義，將重點放在視覺意象的處理上。他在前期以瀟山石為媒材的中國文字作品中，將瀟山石的暗紅以深墨色襯托的看起來有木頭柔韌的質感，而這次的悉曇字則以金色為底，大量覆蓋暗紅色，使得紅色的層次感更加神祕和含蓄，並在光線折射之下，顯出如印材凍石般的意味。

在他掌握幾樣石材的特性和加諸於表面的金色塗佈，使作品的體量感得到寬鬆的釋放。李鎮成如同處理中國文字作品的想法，同樣不改變石材的原本形狀，根據原初的石材形狀僅局部處理稜角和贅材，在較為自然的狀態之下依照不同的形，賦予不同的悉曇字意。一個悉曇字表達眾多的意涵，李鎮成的石材本身的形配合鑲嵌在其中的悉曇符號，形成一個結構體，既有形式意義又有主題的內容，每件作品的標題即是線性符號的悉曇字的漢字翻譯，不懂悉曇字義，可以從作品標題中體會作品可能要傳達的意涵。（參見第56頁《菩提》，2006年作，瀟山石）

結語：回歸生活的平靜

觀看自由造型構成悉曇字這類的作品，著實在我的評論上遭遇了語言的限制顯得障礙重重，在我有限的知識範圍裡，僅僅能提示觀眾李鎮成用有機的組合，使作品充滿李鎮成的願望和某種生活的理想，例如，《娑婆訶》所表示的成就與圓滿吉祥；《觀》與《自在》兩件作品可以組合為一組「觀自在」。其他如，《璀璨》、《興》或《佛法四大天王》組件，是否都能提示一種美好的願望和自我實現的線索呢。

李鎮成戒煙有一段不短的時間了，這位過去的煙友很隨性地說戒就戒，他說「就只是不想抽了。」在我的觀察中，認爲這是與創作一致的生活態度，他原本就有聽佛經、讀佛經，冥想、禪坐的習慣，比較容易知道怎麼去「放下」和「捨得」。他在創作上的執著是堅持自己探索源頭的理念，若是回到他現階段的創作上看，反應自己的生活態度才是一個核心的本質。

李鎮成似乎有一種祈願，希望能回歸更加平靜的心境，從他雕刻《道德經》大型組合式作品開始就能見到他喜歡清靜的端倪，在他現階段運用悉曇文字爲主題中再度看到他依然秉持這樣的願望。如果他體悟世道紛亂，而一直隱於台北塵囂之內，貪看這世間的種種，不過是人的嗔癡使然，李鎮成在作品中表達蘄望大家都能回歸平靜的意願。這或許是他將關心的面相從自己轉化到社會了。

注釋

1 梵字悉曇體字母(Siddha-mātṛka)是約於西元五、六世紀間，流行於北印度的一種梵語書寫文字，原先由笈多(Gupta)字型發展出來，屬婆羅謎(Brāhmī)文字之前北方系型。它由印度經陸路及水路傳入中國、韓國及日本。轉引自，林光明《簡易學梵字》基礎篇，2000，頁18。

2 參見拙作《中國文字的幾種藝術表現──兼論立體文字藝術的新形式》、《塗鴉的自由和嚴肅──試評李鎮成「線性運動」2002塗鴉啓示錄》、《玫瑰戰爭》、《道德經刻石簡介》等文。

3 關於悉曇文的歷史、發展、演變等觀點，均依照林光明先生的研究，我沒有更多能置喙之處。

4 佛教典籍有所謂「一字咒」，通常就是以種子字爲咒。種子字是指用一個字（音節）來代表一位本尊，類似時下年輕人用英文的T表示Tony，或J代表Jennifer。參見林光明《阿彌陀佛一字咒》解讀與結構解析，《咒語漫談電子報》台北：嘉豐出版社。
http://www.dodecyl.com.tw/epaper_022.htm#poem3

5 在西藏密宗寺廟的屋簷、廊下殿角等處，經常可以看到一排排直立的圓木桶或銅鑄的圓桶，較高的有一、二公尺。木製的多爲大紅色，上面刻寫著六字眞言，外有木框、上下有軸，用手輕輕一推即可轉動，藏語稱爲「古拉」。因它面上寫有或內裝有六字大明咒，也稱之爲摩尼桶。

Comment upon
Chen-Cheng Lee's Siddha carving works

By Hu Yi Xun , Associate Professor, Institute of Art Studies, Shanghai University

Preface

When I saw the proper term, "Siddham character" (Siddham), it was quite abstruse and rare to me. Through Chen-Cheng Lee's explanation, I was recalled that some researches mentioned the very character. Yet I had not made any deeper searching inquiry. For us, it is even rarer than those characters of Yunnan's minorities and Tibet. In his recent works, Lee takes this kind of north India's ancient scripts as a subject and creates a series of sculptures which connect with the Buddhist doctrine and wishes for the present lives. Beyond the vision, Lee promotes the language from the shape to the fusion of sounds and meanings.

Through Lee's guidance and introduction, I gradually understand the background of Siddham and enter the subject and the idea of his current creation stage. Further more, I carry on a systematic observation and analyze this kind of works. To analyze Lee's series of Siddham thoroughly, we must relate to his previous sculpture creations which took the Chinese writing as the subject. We will find out whether these two stages have the connection or recent one is a brand-new creation stage. Lee's Chinese script works connect inseparably with his living. Therefore, this article, mainly in the foundation of the author, is discussing Lee's changes of creation style and analyzing his current works.

The Siddham is still unfamiliar to us. If we excessively consume lengths to pick up the scholar's achievements of Siddham studies and verbatim explains the Siddham writing, the main purpose, analyzing and observing Lee's works, will be hindered. Regarding the background such as history, developments, and evolution for Siddham, I extracted parts of the "Easy to learn Sanskrit" written by Lin KuanMing who is an expert in this aspect, in the appendix for reference. The characteristics of Siddham, the limited literary description easily falls into the stumped predicament. As to find the annotation and explanation of his works, paying more attention on shape analysis rather than on meaning explanation is necessary to avoid vague conjecture and essential impairment from too much literary.

Since continuously takes artistic creation, it seems queer for Lee to be interested in Siddham. Neither a philology scholar nor known in the philology domain. Moreover, this kind of north India ancient writing has not been seen as important in Taiwan's academic circles. All seem due to his unreserved action. However, simple reasons can barely explain Lee's systematic creation. It is essential to advanced analyze Lee's initiation idea of choosing his new subject to let us know more about his discovery and works which are originated from a consistent concept.

Shown merely in Buddhism, especially in few studies of Tantric Buddhism, Siddham is esoteric and rare. We can image how difficult for Lee to seek relevant information. He sought Siddham's material through Taiwan's book stores. He also requested his friends in Japan to seek relevant information for him. So he could solve the problem of translation and form the conception for writing performance. All those were important and necessary for him to prepare his creation. Though those endeavors were preparation for his creation, make us experience

Lee's rigorous attitude. He purposed to seek the nutrient and the material which could be displayed in his creation. Lee's main intention is to embark the Buddhist doctrine. For him, the Siddham is one of clues to explore the source.

Speaking of his living background, Lee has studied Buddha for many years. Meditating, burning the Tibetan incense, and reading the Buddhist literature are all in his daily life. Dipping into the Siddham is the result of tracing down the origin of the Buddhist literature and material. Regardless of in his daily life or creation, Lee has his own consistent conviction. "Tracing down the origin" has become the linchpin of his life's journey. He has stockpiled several of stone material at his hometown, Yunlin. He also fully understands the provenance, output, and characteristic of the stone material which has been used in his craving works. To obtain sufficient quantity of specific material for a new work, he once spent three years to trace through its provenance. Such spirit is in accordance with utilizing Siddham, the Buddha writing, as the source of the theme for his works. His mind was occupied by questions as following. What's the source of the sounds for Sanskrit Buddhist literature and Mantra? How to make those peaceful and pure sounds concrete images? Over three years, he gradually found explanations in Siddham.

Lee wields "the seed character" of Siddham. One character contains the meaning of Buddha or Bodhisattva in the Dharma Realm, and also combines "the sound" and "meaning" to manifest the shape. The seed characters are the basic phonetic marks for Siddham, and contain abundant meanings. Lee was probably attracted by this. He explored into in this source not for the Buddhist doctrine but for himself to solves the problem of carving vocabulary. With extremely simple shapes, the Siddham's characters which look like symbols contain the massive Buddhism information. Moreover, those characters can be written in bold and vigorous lines like Chinese calligraphy. For Lee, the complete carving vocabulary, Siddham, was discovered.

Regarding the aspect of creation, Lee took the Chinese writing as the subject of his creation for a period of time. Within his creations, that might be the only connection between Chinese writing and Siddham's characters. It is quite attracting for Lee to find a way to combine shape and meaning of word. Although Lee investigated how Siddham, the northern Indian characters, spread to China, he got more interests in transforming the northern India ancient writing into his creation. Compare to Chinese seal characters, Siddham with more succinct shapes. Meanwhile, each word's meaning is shown by its sound.

New discovery and connection

After studying in the first-phase preparations, Lee has commenced on Siddham's character carving creation since 2005. To show his respects to the Siddham which came of the Buddhist literature origin, Lee's creation abides by the original meaning of each word and emphasizes the image performance of the glyph.

He took Chinese character as the subject for his creation in past ten years. His carving works were transformed from the surface seal cutting form into three-dimensional spatial form. Each stage has its own style characteristic. Since 2005, his Siddham's character creation has seemed back to seal-cutting-like shape vocabulary. However, the creating idea is different from that of his carving work "Daoist Classic" (refer to page 80) ten years ago. He extracted extremely simple denotations from Siddham's characters. Meanwhile, he grasped the writing characteristic, similar to the Chinese seal character, so as to show the Siddham's esthetic shapes by writing and carving. This way is far from reading and expressing in Chinese writing which are familiar to him, and purifies the shape vocabulary. On his carving works, we can see some marks unceasingly duplicated to form line shapes. Lee regularly repeated those marks so as to create harmonious images. To be read is not within his intention for Siddham's works. These writing might indicate a complete concept. Lee's early Chinese writing works contained such intention of being read, nevertheless, in his Sddha series, he dismissed these complex writing reading system (refer to p49, Spell of heart of Infinitely Merciful and Great Compassion Sutra, Liaodong stone 2006).

On the series of miniature works - Manjusri 5-word Sutra (seven pieces in a set), Vajra sattva Mantra (5 pieces in a set), and The Great Compassion Mantra (29 pieces in a set), Lee maintained cube outward appearance though, he actually destroyed the integrity of the cube with Siddham's calligraphy lines. The hollow parts serve as a foil to the entity of lines which make the works not only move on the plane but also shift within three-dimensional space. That makes it necessary to view his works in all directions. On the series of Lee's incantation works, those are like the Tantric Buddhist scripture barrel runner in Tibet. "Those who urge to originate from enlightened mind and rotate the Buddhist scripture barrel may have equivalent merits as chanting all of scriptures."

Xiao Shan stone is one of the stone material in which Lee is skillful to use in his creation. Lee once spent ten years to trace the place of origin of Xiao Shan stone. So that he could have sufficient quantity for creation. Through trial and error for a long time, Lee can master the characteristics of intermediary material. In his Siddham series, Lee selected Xiao Shan stone and the Liaodong stone as two kinds of main materials with sufficient reasons. Xiao Shan stone presents garnet. Liaodong stone and Qingtian stone look like nephrite with green tone. With those two different kinds of materials, Lee not only took advantage of the sedate volume but also utilized their colors to reveal the abundant meanings for Siddham's characters. After being well polished, the garnet Xiao Shan stone and the green Liaodong stone became transparent. In the meantime, weakening the sedate volume made those stones smooth and flexible.

Regarding surface treatment for the stone material, Lee applied the water soluble pigment of the Japanese ukiyoe. Stone material fit with mineral attribute golden dust makes the work full of vitality. Red and gold are the prime colors for Tantric Buddhist in Tibet. Lee did not emphasize the symbolic significance in religiousness but the visual image. In his earlier Chinese writing works, Lee fit garnet Xiao Shan stone with black color so as to make the stone material look like flexible wood. This time, he applied the golden color as the background to make the garnet more mystical and implicit. Under light refracting, those materials appear to be steatites.

By mastering the characteristics of stone materials and spreading golden coating, Lee loosened and released his creations' spirits from heavy and ponderous materials. The treatment was similar to the way he had done on those Chinese writing works before. Lee did not change the original shapes of materials but made partial treatment to get rid of superfluous material. Each work is carved to present certain meanings of Siddham's characters according to the original shape of material. Each Siddham's character contains abundant meanings. Stones with special shapes and the Siddham glyphs construct unique works of great significance. The title for each work is the Chinese translation for the Siddham's character shown on the work. Through each work's title, we can share and experience the idea within Lee's creation, even though we do not know Siddham (refer to p56, Bodhi, Xiao Shan stone 2006).

Conclusion: Return tranquility in life

It is difficult for me to comment on the free style constituted Siddham series. To my limited knowledge, I would like to point out that Lee makes his works full of his wishes and ideas by organic combination. For instance, "svaha" expresses achievement and propitious completion. "Avalokitesvara" includes "Avalokita" and "Isvara". Avalokita means looking and meeting. And Isvara means confort. Others like "Resplendent", "Prosperous" and "Caturmaharajakayikas" sets may provide clues for wonderful wishes and self-actualization.

Lee quit smoking about two years ago. He quit right away when he felt it's the time to quit. To my observation, this attitude is consistent with his creation. Lee is accustomed to reading Buddhist literature and meditation. It is reasonable for him to practice "lay down" and "let go". In creation, he persists in the idea of exploring the source. If we check his recent works, we will find that the core essence for his present works is the reflection to his life attitude.

It seems that Lee has a wish to find the way back to tranquil mood. Through his large scale set work "Daoist Classic", we can find the clue that he does enjoy peaceful life. In his Siddham series of present stage, Lee still present his wish for that. He realizes the world's chaos. Though lives in Taipei, he lives in seclusion to gaze at the dazzling and finds that all are driven by his or her own desires.In his works, Lee expresses his wish for everyone back to tranquil life. That means his concern has been transformed from his own feeling to the society.

書法藝術的新天地——從李鎮成的作品看起

陳聰銘　歷史學博士

　　中國書寫的文化自西方的硬筆發明傳入後，中國人寫字的習慣就發生演變了，硬筆書法也有獨樹一格的審美標準，中國文字總是可以表現出一種架構嚴謹、筆劃流暢的美感。但到了今天，電腦網際網路已成為現代人生活與工作的重心。書寫到一半，突然忘記字句筆劃，或者猛然發覺自己常打電腦鍵盤的手指頭，已經無法找回以往的「筆感」而字跡潦草的體驗，可能是你我時常心生的一種愧疚感，感歎自己筆下的中國文字，相較於傳統書法藝術的筆走龍蛇、壯闊深沉所體現的「形、意、情」最高境界的差距有多少。

　　鎮成兄各階段創作理念的發展脈絡均環環相扣。從早期的「離騷」、「苦熱」，到近年來的「文字皺」，鎮成兄的創作一直在挑戰書法藝術「形、意、情」的界限，這種挑戰並不是要推翻書法藝術的傳統，而是將書法以雕塑的立體形象存在於空間。以「並」字而言，從篆書的兩人手牽手的字體中，形雕成的作品就是兩人緊密地相互扶持，其中所散發出的凝聚力量讓整體的空間更加溫暖與柔和，但同時，也是極為堅牢。所用的石材顏色屬古銅色，更讓人對這作品有一種感觸，似意欲表達彼此扶持的關係是恆久的。另一作品則是「射」字。同樣是篆書，作品以三個重心承接整體的重量，箭矢指向一端，石材為深紅色，有一種深蘊的爆發力，成功地營造出整個作品箭在弦上，蓄勢待發的流暢性與動能。鎮成兄作品將書法藝術立體化、雕塑化和顏色多元化的嘗試，正為這一流傳數千年的藝術注入新的元素。

　　「文字皺」則是透過重覆的字來表現物體的眾多與浩繁，所謂「數大便是美」，藉由墨汁的深淺來顯現遠近層次，筆劃的交錯牽引出連續性，由文字架構出一個延綿不絕、亂中有序、深淺相接的空間，觀者視覺上受到激動，內心的情緒也會隨著畫作邀約進它的氣圍，而穿梭在文字林中與文字共舞了。

　　同出於這條發展脈絡，古印度的梵字也成了創作的靈感來源。雖然不同於中國字的筆劃，但梵字的一筆一劃和其背後的含義，也為他的創作理念作出了另類的詮釋和創作範圍的衍伸。念佛經者經由口中誦念不停的「唵嘛呢叭咪吽」之中，心靈已隨佛音飄送到另一空間的佛祖之處，心神得以淨化。一件上金彩的「吽」字作品就如同「文字皺」般，引靜觀者進入一個心靈的空間，一個物與我相結合的世界。

　　但這並不表示與佛經相關的作品只適合佛教徒的修持經驗，事實上，「靜默」不僅是大多數宗教注重的修練之道，也應是一般忙碌的現代人所需要知道與研習的養身法則，因爲它的修練方法與目的未必與宗教有關，而是在於使一個忙碌的身體與心思能享有片刻的寧靜，讓心靈沉澱下來，體會、思考或追求眞正的「我」，或其他外在事物的本質。

以具有深厚的理論基礎的天主教來說，從二十世紀六〇年代末開始，西方興起一股向東方宗教汲取靈修經驗的浪潮，許多的西方人對佛學和禪學深深著迷。經過研究後，一些神學家與宗教學家發覺東方的靈修方法，可以與西方傳統的基督教靈修法互補；或者以另一種方式說，以基督教爲體，加入東方靈修法爲用。已故的天主教耶穌會著名的漢學家甘易逢（Yves Raguin, s.j., 1912-1998）神父認爲：

『基督宗教與其他宗教相遇，可使我們以新的眼光看我們的信仰；別人之所信會讓我們反省自己之所信。這不是宗教融合，而是啓示的發展。』（請參閱甘易逢，「靜觀與默坐」之四）。

修持者的宗教信仰爲何並不是重點，靜默的目的只是在於如何在靈修的路上不會被雜念或邪念誤導。

雖然鎭成兄的梵字刻石以佛經來呈現他的創作理念，但這只是一個引子，對非佛教徒而言，內心依然空靈自由，任自己摸索內在的世界；對佛教徒而言，更可從觀賞和觸摸作品之中，猶如手轉法輪般，領悟由佛祖流傳下來的古老、深奧的法語，啓示自己的佛性。

鎭成兄這些年來的努力與嘗試，已跨越了傳統的書法藝術所揭櫫的「形、意、情」之標準，並直指人的心靈深處，達到「物體與心靈合一」的境地，從「形、意、情、靈」這四個角度，應該可以用比較完整的視野來觀賞他的作品。

The New World of the Art of Calligraphy:
Observation on the Works of Chen-Cheng Lee

By Chen Tsung-ming, Ph.D. Alexander

Since the introduction of pen from the West to the East, the Chinese people gradually changed their traditional way of writing. The calligraphy of pen has its own esthetic criterion. However, nobody can deny that the Chinese characters always show a finely esthetic feature combining strict structure and fluent traits. Nevertheless, computer and internet dominate an important part of everybody's daily life in the modern society. It sometimes occurs that we forget certain parts of characters while writing; or suddenly, we find that the fingers, having become used to the computer keyboard, can feel no longer the "good touch of pen", and so form awkward words. We can be ashamed of our own characters which are surely far away from the calligraphic ideal : "forms, meanings and feelings".

Chen-Cheng's inspiration in different phases is tightly linked to one another. From his works of early years: "Lisao", "Heat", and his recent creations in the Tsuen Calligraphy, his creativity seems to challenge the top limits of "forms, meanings and feelings". This challenge is never to overthrow the long tradition of calligraphic art, but to seek to dress this art in a three-dimensional form integrated into an open space. To give an example, "Together" is a work which is structured by the ancient pictorial script "Zhuan", with the feature of two persons hand in hand. The cohesion which is spreading out of this sculpture keeps the whole space warm, soft and solid. The color of this piece is bronze, which can give an image of a long and lasting relationship. Another piece is "Shooting". Formed as well according to the script of Zhuan on a deep red stone, this work is supported by three canters of gravity. Its head of arrow hoards a potential power ready for shooting. Chen-Cheng Lee endeavors consist to relief, to sculpt and to color the calligraphic art. The fruit of the tentative adds fresh new elements to this art evaluating throughout for thousands years.

The Tsuen Calligraphy demonstrates the expansion and the complexity of the same word through brush strokes which spread fully on the painting. We can find out that our optical nerves are stimulated by the organization of the painting. The combination of light and dark ink show the distance of objects; crossing lines lead to continuity. Characters construct a breathing space amidst continuity, an order in chaos and a connection between light and dark colors. Our feeling is invited by the painting to enter into the atmosphere of its forest and dance with the characters.

Being in this same context of the creative line, the traditional Sanskrit characters also inspired his creativity to form sculptured stones. Although the Sanskrit characters differ from the structure of the Chinese characters, their traits and meaning inspired Li's motivation and expanded his field of the creativity. Following the recitation of the canonistic works of Buddhism, the Buddhists' spirit is sent to the Buddha, and thus gets purified. The gold work on the Sanskrit character of "hong" is just like the "function" of the tsuen calligraphy, which leads us to a spiritual space, a world of a union between the object and me.

Nevertheless, this doesn't mean that the works concerning the Buddhism can only be suited for the Buddhists' experience of self-training. "Meditation" is not only a principle of self-training for believers in most of religions, but also an important way for maintaining the health of everybody in modern society. Its method and objective are not necessary linked with religious conviction, but are also linked with the pursuit of a complete and momentary calm, in which a tired and busy body - soul relaxes in order to feel, rethink or search for the real ego, or the true nature of a material object.

As an example from Catholicism, since the end of 1960's in the Western world, people are attracted by the experiences of meditation in the Eastern religions. Many Western persons are fascinated by Buddhism and Zen. After some studies, some theologians and experts find that the approach of the Eastern meditation can be useful for the traditional Western spirituality. In other words, Christianity is the structure and the Eastern way of meditation will serve as an approach. The deceased Jesuit priest, Yves Raguin, s.j. (1912-1998) estimated:

"The encounter between the Christianity and other religions allows us to have a new vision of our own conviction. That in which the others believe will make ourselves proceed to reflection upon that in which we believe. This is by no means a fusion of religions, but a development of enlightenment." (cf. Y. Raguin, contemplation and Sitting in Silence, vol. IV, Chinese Spirituality)

The trainee's conviction is not the point. The aim of the meditation consists in the use of a compass for him to avoid misguidance by worldly, even evil thoughts.

Although Chen-Cheng Lee expresses his creativity through some sculpted stones of Sanskrit script, the approach is a simple catalyst. For the non-Buddhists, their mind is rendered disposable and free enough to explore their inner life. Through exposure to the sculptured works, the Buddhists can perceive the old and profound dharma, and thus illumine their own true Nature revealed by Buddhism.

Chen-Cheng's efforts and attempts throughout these years exceed effectively the criterion, "forms, meaning and feelings", which is claimed by traditional calligraphic art, and appeal directly to one's soul. This appeal can reach the frontier of "union between object and mind". From the four aspects, "forms, meanings, feelings and spirit", we will be able to have a comprehensive view to appreciate his works.

愛的夠深～李鎮成～無所不能

高愛倫　湯臣娛樂執行長

　　「愛的夠深」，好像是一個很生刻的字眼，但是對李鎮成而言，「愛的夠深」，只是熱烈回應生活、生存、生命的基本態度，仰賴著這四個字，他雕琢了愛情、他也雕琢了藝術，他雕琢了夢想、他也雕琢了理想。

　　李鎮成是雲林農家子弟，即便他還是個孩子的時候，他就懂得把嗜好綁在空閒的時間上，讓自己的心靈始終閃耀著飽滿的喜樂。

　　白天，李鎮成赤足踩在田裡幹活。
　　黃昏，李鎮成在田埂或休憩的茅草屋裡繪畫、寫字。
　　晚上，李鎮成刻圖章娛樂。

　　透過這樣的童年歲月，「性格」演變成「風格」、「特別」種植出「特色」，只是喜歡玩泥、玩石、玩墨的初衷，終在李鎮成內在形成更巨大的力道，當他還來不及決定做一個藝術家的時候，他已經是一個不折不扣的藝術工作者。

　　李鎮成一向不相信一見鍾情這等文藝腔的故事，然而，一次聚會的初遇，讓他發狂了。但是：

　　他，高中畢業，她，大學碩士。
　　他，來自鄉下，她，祖籍浙江。
　　他，身高168，她，身高163。

　　「誠實與誠懇」＋「熱情與熱烈」＝李鎮成的魅力

　　那個叫羅麗珍的女孩，從一開始就知道自己遇到了幸福，可是她的家庭卻陷入無從理解的惡夢。

　　好在，他的天秤座總是讓自己有平衡點，她的巨蟹座總是讓自己有期待感。

　　歷經八年的努力，李鎮成終於跨越門檻，得到婚姻的祝福；從此，他完全折服自己的座右銘：「愛的夠深，什麼都能」。

　　十個藝家九個霸，因為印象總是這麼說的：情緒衝突越大，作品跳躍度越高。

　　李鎮成可不欣賞假借藝術之名偏好的自虐，他說：「創作，的確有過程上的痛苦，但不該是由他人陪同受苦」。

　　羅麗珍主修園藝、嗜愛美術設計，她順他、她膩他、她寵他，李鎮成唯一的責任就是專注油畫、文字刻石、書法的創作，幾度藝展的專刊都是由羅麗珍編輯完稿，當他們意見不一致的時候，李鎮成的心裡就想起一個聲音：家庭和諧、家庭和諧......。他們都明白：不退讓、不謙讓，不意味是正確的堅持，所以多聽對方的聲音，可以讓作品的呈現更人性、更柔軟。

「創作需要體力。」所以現階段，李鎮成把坐寫書法、立繪油畫的至愛暫且降溫，當作怡情養性的自修，而全力以攻的是石雕之藝，「我喜歡挑戰石頭的硬度，相對的，我也在挑戰自己面對頑石的耐度：一塊石頭從切割、脬光、雕刻，每一個過程都是以力氣搏鬥創意。」

因為耗力太多，加上切割刀控制不易，李鎮成在創作日的每一個工作日，幾乎都是汗濕淋漓如水人，身上也常有跑刀的傷痕，我問他，為什麼會選這麼勞頓、勞苦的創作類型？他想也不想，很自然的就引用他的經典答案：「愛的夠深，什麼都能。」

在一對一的對話空間裡，李鎮成可以從別人的討論中興發評論自己作品的話題，既可不拘束的表達創作意念與意圖，也能不計褒貶的專心傾聽視聽感受，但是在藝展的現場，他卻格外沉靜。

他的內斂可能是源於一個理論：「藝術不是在人群中喊話、藝術是與知己的知心對話。」

我跟李鎮成談話的感覺很好：這個人，十足的是藝術家，又十足的不是藝術家。

談創作時，李鎮成像海浪，翻騰澎湃，氣勢探天。

談生活時，李鎮成像水舞，光影婆娑，剛柔交錯。

Anything is Possible
with Deep Enough Love

By Allen Kao, CEO of Tomson Entertainment Company

"To love deep enough" sounds like a very profound phrase but to Chen-Cheng Lee, "to love deep enough" is his enthusiastic response and his basic attitude towards living, survival and life. He carves love, art, dreams and ideals relying on the four words.

Chen-Cheng Lee is from a farming family in Yunlin and when he was a child he understood how to tie his hobbies to his leisure time so that his heart and spirits always sparkled with abundant joy.

By day, Chen-Cheng Lee worked on the rice field with his bare feet.
At sunset, Chen-Cheng Lee drew and wrote at the ridge of the rice field or in a hut.
By night, Chen-Cheng Lee carved seals for recreation.

Through such a childhood, "personality" has evolved into "style" and "uniqueness" has grown into "characteristics". The initial liking to play with mud, rock and ink has become an even more powerful force within Chen-Cheng Lee so that he was already an art maker through and through when he was yet to decide to become an artist.

Chen-Cheng Lee never believed in cliché stories such as love at first sight but a chance encounter made him crazy with love.

He is a high school graduate and she has a Master's degree.
He is from the country and her ancestral home is Zhejiang.
He is 168 c.m. tall, she is 163 c.m. tall.

"Honesty and sincerity"+ "passion and enthusiasm" = Chen-Cheng Lee's charm.

The girl named Janet Lo knew from the beginning that she has found her happiness but her family was plunged into an incomprehensible nightmare.

Luckily, as a Libra he always finds his balance, and as a Cancer she always gives herself something to expect.

After eight years of hard work, Chen-Cheng Lee finally crosses the threshold and gains blessings for their marriage and after that he is a firm believer of his motto "anything is possible by loving deep enough."

Nine out of ten artists are fierce as I recall a saying: the more intense the emotional conflict is, the more vibrant the work is.

Chen-Cheng Lee, however, does not appreciate self-abuse in the name of appreciating the art. He says: "The creating process is indeed painful but others should not have to share the suffering."

Janet Lo majors in gardening and loves graphics design. She obeys him, adores him and dotes on him and Chen-Cheng Lee's only responsibility is to focus on oil painting, stone carving and calligraphy. Janet Lo is in charge of editing the publications for his several exhibitions and when they have difference in opinions, there is a voice ringing in Chen-Cheng Lee's heart: family harmony, family harmony... They both understand that refusing to compromise or back down does not mean insisting on the right side so listening more to each other's voice can make a work more human and tender.

"Creating needs strength." So at the present stage Chen-Cheng Lee cools down his passion for calligraphy and oil painting as a pastime to sooth one's spirits and nourish one's nature in order to focus on stone carving. "I like to challenge the hardness of a stone and on the other hand, I am also challenging my own patience on a stubborn stone, from cutting a stone to polishing and carving it, each process is a struggle between creativity and strength."

Because such work consumes too much strength and it is not easy to control the chisel, Chen-Cheng Lee is sweaty like a man made of water during his workdays and he usually bears the marks from his injuries. I asked him why choosing such a laborious and painful type of creation, he quoted his classic answer without thinking: "Anything is possible with deep enough love."

In a one-on-one dialogue, Chen-Cheng Lee can freely review his works to express his ideals and intentions and listen carefully to the other's feedback without worrying about being praised or criticized but he is unusually quiet on the scene of an exhibition.

His restraint may come from a theory: "Art is not shouting to a crowd, art is conducting a heartfelt dialogue with those who appreciate it."

I feel very good when I am in a dialogue with Chen-Cheng Lee, he is a pure artist and purely not an artist.

When talking about creation, Chen-Cheng Lee is like the waves, churning and surging with a momentum reaching the sky.

When talking about life, Chen-Cheng Lee is like dancing water, a swirl of light and shadow and a blend of steel and tenderness.

中華文化的精髓在台灣—李鎮成的藝術人生

胡雪紅

1998年國立故宮博物院，「從傳統中創新」李鎮成文字雕塑展，那年，他36歲。

父母、兄姐、師長的愛，成就了李鎮成對藝術的想望。

李鎮成，1962年生於台灣雲林縣莿桐鄉甘西村。世代務農，在家中排行第五。父親的開明教育孕育了三個兒子的藝術志趣，不同於一般孩子的玩耍嬉戲，畫畫、雕刻、讀帖、臨帖、雙鉤白描填紅占據了李鎮成大部分的年少時光。

從小到大，無論學校或家裡都給了李鎮成極大的創作自由：上課時間，他有特權在田野間盡情寫生；在家裡，他把就讀嘉義師專美勞科的大哥帶回給弟妹們的習字字帖拆開，貼滿四壁與天花板，學和尚打坐讀經的氣勢，讓碑帖的精神漸漸地從生活中滲透入每一個細胞。其中，他特別偏愛「玉筋篆」向樹幹般自然轉折的中鋒線條，也引發了日後對大篆、毛公鼎、散氏盤與大小克鼎的興趣。為了省錢，父親從鄉公所載回一疊疊的舊報紙供他瘋狂練字，一張報紙寫一個大字的氣魄，用深淺不同的墨色反覆使用直到不能用為止。

1977年，台北故宮博物院展出「晚明變形主義畫家作品展」，大哥認為李鎮成擁有和這些畫家極其相似的靈魂，特地帶他北上參觀，還買了一本定價900元的昂貴畫冊送給他當作國中畢業禮物。那次觀展所造成心靈的衝擊與震撼，深深影響日後李鎮成的藝術創作。21年後，李鎮成既傳統又有新意的文字雕刻作品，受到前故宮博物院院長秦孝儀先生所賞識，親自安排展出。再度來到國家最高藝術殿堂，除了覺得莫大的榮耀，更對大哥當年的提攜，感念有加。從事藝術創作對李鎮成而言是一種天命。

1973年台日斷交的第二年，棄農從商的父親所經營的食品工廠倒閉，家中經濟陷入絕境，債主天天上門討債。看盡人情冷暖，少年李鎮成暗自發誓要用自己的方式出人頭地。

雕刻，是小時候陪爸爸務農的娛樂之一。春播前，父親犁土翻起的土塊，李鎮成用竹片、鐵釘、小刀刻成栩栩如生的小動物們，還曾雕了一座觀音像，回家偷放在神明廳的供桌上，裝米插香，膜拜一番，傳為家中笑談。

高中時，李鎮成隨虎尾高中賈松珍老師習國畫、書法，見老師刻印大感興趣。視鎮成如子的賈老師，送了一塊如肥皂大小的壽山石與一把刻刀給他，李鎮成如獲至寶，從此開啟了李鎮成的篆刻生涯。

從小，李鎮成學業成績不盡理想，課本上畫滿了雙鉤白描的三國、水滸人物。不過，他是書法、繪畫比賽的常勝軍，讀高中時的國文老師也來跟他學習書法。高二那年參加全國國語文競賽書法類比賽，烏龍報名成為社會組，竟然得到第二名。1980年，18歲的李鎮成獲得日本東京都美術館書法展「秀作」獎的殊榮。 他一直努力朝藝術的理想前進。

造化弄人，不知是幸或不幸，大學聯考，學科成績過關，書法比賽的常勝軍在書法科目卻破天荒僅得2分！李鎮成抑鬱悲憤莫名，學院夢碎。然而，卻意外開啓了他日後自我學習，從創作中追求知識，在實作與理論的反覆驗證中，摸索出屬於自己獨特風格的創作道路。

聯考落榜，單調的軍旅生活，李鎮成寄情於文學，書法，刀法，皴法。把對現實的絕望移情至他鍾愛的礦石上。落寞寡歡的李鎮成，把帶去軍中的印石，刻了又磨，磨了又刻，藉以抒發心中的鬱悶，沒想到因此奠下篆刻深厚的基本功。有一天，基於愛石、惜石之心，李鎮成把一方泰來石印章的六個面，全部刻滿了他所愛的篆字，新的意象讓他興奮不已，意外地開啓了他文字雕刻的創作大門，也為日後的立體文字刻石藝術奠定了重要的基礎。

1983—1994，李鎮成人生最困頓的黑暗時期。

1983年，對李鎮成影響最深的父親病逝，軍中請假未准，無法見父親最後一面。退役後，短暫回到南部老家開班教授小朋友與社會人士書法與繪畫。才藝班經營不善，隔年關門大吉。1987年，羅麗珍—李鎮成藝術生命中最重要的陪伴與支持者，相識於李鎮成二哥的婚禮上。碩士學歷，任教於文化大學園藝系。天差地遠的生活背景，讓他們的交往受到女方父母強烈反對。

一連串的不順遂之下，1988年李鎮成離家北上，在陽明山國家公園附近一處由豬舍改建的鐵皮小屋中，過著與世隔絕，自我放逐的日子。

如同許多對藝術懷抱著理想，卻在現實生活中載浮載沉的青年一樣，李鎮成用豐富的創作力寄情、抒懷，用藝術國度的溫暖美好，對抗人世的現實悲苦。

陽明山大自然的力量撫慰著李鎮成的心靈，也提供日後李鎮成的油畫創作源源不盡的靈感：中國古文學中，屈原的《天問》與《離騷》和他的心境相應和著！ 李鎮成選擇了緻密、細膩、堅韌的端石，每天衝刀、推刀，埋首創作，歷時一年，先後完成了【天問】(17件)與【離騷】(24件)兩套作品。

除了石刻，不能忘情於水墨的李鎮成，這段期間也開始了充滿衝突、掙扎、「悲愴系列」人物水墨創作。

1989年，母親北上接回身心俱疲的兒子。

炎夏裡，甘西村的鐵皮屋中，李鎮成將大石立起雕刻，完成了第一件立體石雕—王維的【苦熱】。

1992年，母親驟逝，有很長一段時間李鎮成封閉自己。讀佛經、聽梵唱成了情緒宣洩的出口，亦埋下了後來【悉曇文】系列的創作種子。

家人朋友相伴的藝術創作路

一切的磨難似乎在1995年以後告一段落。經過八年的堅持與努力，李鎮成終於得到岳父岳母的同意，在聖誕夜與羅麗珍完成終身大事。

有情人終成眷屬，李鎮成的藝術生命得到空前的鼓舞。他的創作不再單單是對自己的生命吶喊，也是與知己的知心對話。詩品與禪偈的刻石系列，皆取材於妻子喜愛的詩詞歌賦。兩年後，女兒牧芸出生，重新回到家庭懷抱的李鎮成，有感而發，做出《說文解字》系列第一件作品【家】。

1996，李鎮成在彩田藝術空間發表首次個展。其後，李鎮成推陳出新，創作不斷，幾乎年年都有作品展出，展歷遍及故宮博物院、歷史博物館、國父紀念館等國家級藝術寶殿。

1997，前故宮博物院院院長秦孝儀先生，親臨敦煌藝術中心參觀李鎮成「空間中行走的文字」個展，當場邀請李鎮成到故宮博物院展出，促成了1998故宮「從傳統中創新」的文字雕塑展，使李鎮成成為國內少數擁有故宮博物院展歷的年輕藝術創作者。

藝術是一條苦其心志、勞其筋骨的坎坷路。家，是李鎮成創作的堡壘，家人，是他精神的支柱，還有來自各方好友的真心相助。有家人的陪伴與朋友的支持，李鎮成把對自己生命內在的經驗、記憶、渴望與幻想，透過創作一一呈現，繼續著對藝術的熱愛與執著。

文字雕刻─最具人類思維特性的視覺藝術

選擇「文字」作為創作的主軸，根源於幼時對讀帖、臨帖的狂熱，書法飛揚的線條與意境早已成為李鎮成骨血的一部份。

文學，乘載了古往今來人類的思想與情感。文學的基本元素是文字，透過視覺的閱讀，文字轉換為思維或情感的表達。

篆刻，是以文字為基礎，以雕刻為表現的藝術形式。

李鎮成的文字刻石融合了文學的意境，書法線條的觸感，天然石材的色澤溫潤多變，還有三度空間的立體呈現。李鎮成的刻石創作有別於篆刻，不同於石雕，挑戰著「形」、「意」、「情」的極限。觀賞、撫觸、沉思，李鎮成的文字雕刻可以說是最具人類思維的視覺藝術。

創作思維

李鎮成立體刻石的靈感，來自於古印度的佛塔與馬雅文化的文字塔。他說：「手指的觸感是長久以來我所追求的。好比我們爬山時，摸著岩石，一路上行的感覺。」「亨利摩爾與羅丹在作雕塑時，會有面的變化，我相信篆刻脫胎換骨之後，中國文字也可以做到。」

李鎮成懂石、愛石成癡。觸摸審視石材的形狀、弧度、色澤、姿態，想像著最能與之搭配詮釋的詩詞文章，將文字作為視覺符號，把印面篆刻的處理，隨著手指的觸感，轉化成為整體的有機構成。

書法是李鎮成的最愛。「文字皺」的發想，衍生自長期以來李鎮成對書法線條的均衡、佈局、空間、速度，甚至墨的濃淡乾濕之探索，進而將書法文字當成「繪畫元素」，在作品上構築山水意象。

李鎮成的文字皺，整體的繪畫性意象強過書法，後來發展出平面的書法系列與立體的刻石系列。

　　1989年的【苦熱】是李鎮成最早的文字皴系列雕塑作品，篆體文字佈滿山型的泰來石，試圖將文字單純地作爲一種視覺符號的表象。後來的【道德經】刻石系列(1992—1994)到最近的【千字文】與【悉曇文】刻石系列(2004—2008)，都延續了將文字作爲視覺符號的創作理念。

結語

　　無邊界的創作理念，李鎮成的文字藝術兼具台灣本土精神與中華文化精髓，既傳統又有新意，有文化的底蘊又令人驚艷不已。

　　2008年7月，國立歷史博物館，「字在無邊—李鎮成文字藝術展」，李鎮成最新創作成果，靜待各界指教。

The Essence of Chinese Culture in Taiwan:
Chen-Cheng Lee's artistic life

By Amy Hu

In 1998, at the age of 36, Chen-Cheng Lee's writing sculpture works were exhibited in "New Trends in Chinese Traditional Fine Arts", National Palace Museum.

Love from family and schoolmasters fulfilled Chen-Cheng Lee's Vision of arts.

Chen-Cheng Lee was born in 1962, grew up at Gan Xi village, Cihtong town, Yunlin County, Taiwan. His family has been engaged in agriculture for generations. He is the fifth child in the family. His father's enlightened education has bred three son's artistic interests. Unlike other children, Lee spent most of his young time in painting, carving, studying and practicing the writing, and sketch etc...

Lee has been given enormous freedom for creation by his family and schools since he was a little boy. In the school hours, Lee was given the privilege to paint from nature in the field. At home, he tore off each page of his calligraphy book and glued those pages on four walls and the ceiling. Those books were brought back by his elder brother who studied at Jia-yi normal junior college at that time. Lee learned the imposing manners which the Buddhist priests did in meditation and Buddhist literature studying. So the spirit from those stone inscriptions can gradually permeate through his creation life and cells. His most favorite was the "Jade Ligament Seal Style" of which lines looked like natural boughs' intricateness. That also initiated his interest in the big seal, Mao-kung Ting, and San P'an. For the sake of money saving, his father carries a pack of old newspaper from the township hall for him to practice calligraphy. To show the breadth of spirit, Lee wrote one large brush-written Chinese character on one piece of newspaper. He also wrote on same paper repeatedly with ink of different depth until that paper could not be used anymore.

In 1977, "Exhibition of Latter Ming dynasty distortion principle painters' works" was held in the National Palace Museum. His eldest brother thought Lee's artistic soul was similar to that of those painters. For that special purpose, his eldest brother led him to the exhibition and bought him an expensive picture album as a gift for celebrating his graduation from junior high school. That exhibition caused impact and shock on Lee's mind and brought deep influence in his artistic creation. After 21 years, Chen-Cheng Lee's writing sculpture works which with tradition and fresh idea attracted the recognition from former National Palace Museum Director Dr. Ch'in Hsiao-yi. Dr. Ch'in invited and arranged Chen-Cheng Lee to exhibit his writing sculpture works in the National Palace Museum. It's the greatest honor for Lee to have his won exhibition in the highest art palace. Besides, he felt grateful with all his heart to his eldest for his touching leading.

For Chen-Cheng Lee, engaging in artistic creation is a kind of destiny

In 1973, the year after breaking off diplomatic relations between Taiwan and Japan, the food factory of Chen-Cheng Lee's father who was once a farmer and tried to run a business went into bankruptcy. The financial situation of his family fell into dilemma and those creditors dunned them for payment daily. After recognizing the grim reality, young Chen-Cheng Lee pledged his word secretly to become outstanding in his own way.

Carving was one of entertainment in Lee's childhood accompanied by his father who worked at farm. Before the spring sowing, his father plowed and turned soil block. Lee engraved little lifelike animals with bamboo strip, nail, and knives. He once carved a statue of Buddha, put on the table and worshiped it. His family thought that for a joke.

Lee learned and practiced the traditional Chinese painting and the calligraphy from his teacher, Mr. Song-Jen Ja, in Hu-Wei senior high school. Lee was interested in Mr. Ja's engraving. Mr. Ja, had seen Lee as his own child, gave him a soap size agalmatolite and a burin. Lee was so happy as if he had found the most valuable treasure. Lee began his seal craving profession from that time on.

Lee's school grades was not good when he was a child. There're always full of outline drawings of different stories' figures on his textbooks. Though, he often won championship in calligraphy and drawing competitions. Even teachers came to him for learning calligraphy when he was in senior high school. In his 11th grade, he attended the national calligraphy competition. Due to a entry mistake, his name was entered in the social group. To every one's surprise, he won the second prize. In 1980, when he was 18 year old, Chen-Cheng Lee won the "Excellence prize" in the calligraphy exhibition of Tokyo Metropolitan Art Museum, Japan. He makes every effort to fulfill his artistic dream continuously.

The god of destiny seemed to made fools of him. Unfortunately, in the college entrance examination, Lee was qualified in academic criteria and yet failure in the subject of calligraphy, though he was the champion of calligraphy competition. Lee became extremely angry and depressed. The way to academic learning seemed to be obstructed. However, the event unexpectedly opened his own way to study and practice by himself in the future. Lee has obtained knowledge from creating. Through the process of practices and repeat theories verifications, Lee has tried to find out his own style of creation.

When he was in flunk the entrance examination for college admission and the drab of military life, Chen-Cheng Lee expressed his feelings by literature, calligraphy, carving knife skills, and the method of showing texture of rocks. Since he was disappointed in reality, Leetransferred his enthusiasm to the stone carving. Lee, lonely and desolate, engraved those stones and later rubbed off again and again so as to express his oppression. Unexpectedly, those practices laid the foundation for the seal carving. One day, because of treasuring the stone material, Lee engraved completely six surfaces on a Tailai stone full of his favorite writing characters. The new image made him felt excited and accidentally opened the road of his writing carving creation. That also laid the significant foundation for his later creation of three-dimensional writing sculpture.

1983-1994, Chen-Cheng Lee's most exhausted and darkest days in his lifetime

In 1983, Lee's father who had the most important influence on Lee passed away. Since the request for leave was not been permitted, Lee was unable to accompanied his father at his last days. After released from military service, Lee returned to his hometown to run a workshop and to teach calligraphy and the drawing. The workshop wasn't well managed and then closed down. In 1987, at Lee's brother's wedding ceremony, he was acquainted with Ms. Janet Lo, the most important company and supporter in Lee's life. Janet owns a Master degree. She was an Instructor at the department of horticulture, Chinese Culture University. The enormous difference of life background made the parents of Janet intensely opposed their affections.

After experienced a series of misfortunes, Chen-Cheng Lee left home and head for Taipei in 1988. He lived at a small hut which had been a hoggery and closed to the Yangmingshan National Park. He lived an isolated and exiled life.

Like other young artists who embrace their dreams yet cannot afford stable lives in reality, Chen-Cheng Lee expressed his roaring feeling and passions with the abundant creation and resisted the sorrowful reality with the warmth and beautifulness.

The nature power from Yang-ming mountain comforted Lee's wounded heart. Moreover, it provided endless inspiration for Lee in his later oil painting series. In the Chinese ancient literature, these poems "Li Sao: Suffering Throes" and "Verse on the Heaven" by the ancient poet Qu Yuan could find an echo in Lee's heart. Chen-Cheng Lee has chosen compactly, smooth, and tenacious Tuan stone to be the material. During one year, he created with all his energy. He completed the series of "Verse on the Heaven" (17 pcs) and "Li Sao: Suffering Throes" (24 pcs).

Not only stone carving, but also ink painting attracted Chen-Cheng Lee. In these days, he began the series of figure ink painting named "Grief" in which full of conflicts, struggles, and distortion.

In 1989, Lee's mother went to pick up her beloved son and brought him home. Lee was exhausted in body and mind at that time. At those hot summer days, in the iron-covered hut of his hometown, Chen-Cheng Lee set up a large stone and carved. Then he completed his first three-dimensional stone carving, Heat, which named after the poem of Tang Dynasty poet Wang Wei.

In 1992, Lee's mother suddenly passed away. That had caused him to isolate himself from others for a long time. During that time, reading the Buddhist literature and listening to the Buddhist songs became the outlet for his mood and also laid down the seed for creating his Siddham series afterwards.

Art creation along with family and friends.

All tribulations seemed to come to the end in 1995. After eight year's insistence and diligently, Lee finally got the approval from Janet's parents and married her on the Christmas Eve.

Two lovers finally became one couple. That did infuse and inspire Lee's artistic life. His creation is not only to cry his heart out but also to dialogue with whom beloved. Those series of poems and Zen gathas were all from his wife's favorite poems and gathas. Their daughter, Mu-Yun was born two years later. Since regained the warmth of family, Lee created his work named "Home" which was the first work of the "Origin of the Chinese Characters" series.

In 1996, Chen-Cheng Lee held his first solo exhibition at the "Pan Pan Art Space". Since then, Lee brings forth the new through the old. His creations are unceasing. He has new art works to be exhibited every year. His exhibitions were held in those State-level art palaces, like National Palace Museum, National Museum of History, and National Dr. Sun Yat-sen Memorial Hall etc...

In 1997, former National Palace Museum Director Dr. Ch'in Hsiao-yi came to Lee's solo exhibition "Writing walking on the space" in Caves Art Center. Dr. Ch'in invited Lee to hold exhibition in the National Palace Museum. That facilitated Lee's writing sculpture works to be exhibited in "New Trends in Chinese Traditional Fine Arts", in the National Palace Museum, 1998. Chen-Cheng Lee is one of few young artists who has the experience of exhibition in the National Palace Museum.

As an artist, art creation is a rugged path which is physical and mental exhausted. His home is the fortress for his creation. His family is his spirit props. And those sincere assistances from friends are also important to him. With the supports of family and friends, Lee continues his passion on arts and transforms his inner experiences, memories, desires, and illusions to visible arts works.

Writing sculptures, one of the most important visual arts with the significant performance of humanity's thoughts.

It has its source in the passion for studying and practicing the writing in childhood, Chen-

Cheng Lee took the writing as the subject of his art works. Writing with ease and smooth lines and poetry like realm has become part of Lee's life.

Literature carries humanity's thoughts and emotions throughout the ages. Writing is one of fundamental elements for literature. Writing has been transformed into the thoughts and emotions by visual reading.

Seal cutting is an artistic form which bases on character and writing and manifests itself through engraving.

Chen-Cheng Lee's writing sculptures integrate calligraphy line touch with literature thought. Through his art works, we can enjoy the diversity of stone material and be amazed by the appearance of three-dimension. Lee's writing sculptures are far beyond seal cutting and different from stone carving. Moreover, through those works, Lee tried his best to challenge himself to the limitation of "forms", "meanings", and "images. Chen-Cheng Lee's writing sculpture is one of the most important visual arts with the significant performance of humanity's thoughts.

Thoughts of Creation

Chen-Cheng Lee's three-dimensional sculptures were inspired by the the ancient India's pagoda and the Maya culture writing tower. "Finger-toughing feeling is what I have been pursuing. It is just like when we go mountain climbing, our hands touch the stones laying on the trail side when we go uphill. When Henry Moore and Auguste Rodin were doing their sculptures, they would do surface variation, thus, I believe that seal carving could be thoroughly remold, and once this is achieved, Chinese characters could reach new heights.", Lee said.

Chen-Cheng Lee understands those characters of different kinds of stones and loves them. He can image the best poetry and written articles to match different stones by touching and examining shape, radian, luster, and posture of those stones. He utilizes writing characters to be visual symbols, along with the finger touch, so as to transform the surfaces of seal cutting into an organic structure as a whole.

The idea of "Calligraphy-Tsuen" was initiated from Lee's long-term exploration of calligraphic lines. That included exploring the equilibrium, the layout, the space, and the speed of lines; and exploring the darkness and humidness of ink.   Then he took the calligraphy writing as the drawing elements and constructed the scenery image on his works.

Overall, the image of the Calligraphy-Tsuen series is pictorial rather than calligraphic. Afterward he developed the plane calligraphy series and three-dimensionally stone carving series.

"Heat" is Lee's earliest work of the Calligraphy-Tsuen series. He carved seal characters on mountain shape Tailai stone. He attempted to use writing characters as pure visual symbols. His later works of "Tao Te Ching" series and recent "Thousand Character Essay" series and "Shiddha" series also extended the same concept.

Conclusion

Lee's concept of creation is borderless. His works of script art possess Chinese cultural essence as well as Taiwan native spirits, fresh idea as well as tradition, impressiveness as well as cultural reality.

July 2008, at National Museum of History, Lee's solo exhibition "Borderless Calligraphy" is waiting for your presence and comments.

悉曇文刻石

Sculpture
of Siddham

悉曇文（Siddham）是公元第五至第六世紀流行於北印度的梵語書寫文字。 南北朝末期傳入中國。隋唐時代佛教興盛，梵文是當時中國最流行的外國語言之一，當時所稱的梵文實際即悉曇文字；佛教經典多以這種文字寫成。悉曇字後來在印度隨著佛教的沒落與蒙古人入侵而漸漸不再被使用，在中國也逐漸為蒙古文和西藏文所取代。

在日本悉曇字則因密宗佛教的流行而一直使用到今天。除了宗教因素外，日本人把悉曇字當作一種藝術來學習和欣賞；隨著時代環境演變，悉曇字的藝術性逐漸勝過宗教性，進而發展出帶有審美意義的悉曇書法 。漢字之外，世界上再沒有一種文字像悉曇字這樣被賦如此豐富而多采的藝術審美精神的。由於日本人發展出悉曇書法審美價值與系統，使悉曇書法超越宗教與語言的界線，成為人類共同的重要藝術文化資產。

李鎮成其長期投入的文字藝術創作，一直探討漢字的藝術性本質。基本上李鎮成對文字是非常敏感的，悉曇字之所以吸引他首先便是其文字本身婉轉多姿的藝術性；其宗教性反而是次要的。 李鎮成一直是以全副的生命及他對生命的嚴肅態度從事藝術創作。他創作的文字藝術尤其多一分虔誠與尊敬。他在「悉曇系列」中精進學習，其作品予人們一種無限的祥和及寧靜感；正如「悉曇」一詞的本義，是一種互證的圓滿，也是一種自證的成就。

心經咒語 Spell of Heart Sutra

2005, 3 X 3 X 7 cm, 17 pcs
青田石 Stone，共17件

以悉曇文為創作元素，表現書法的韻律和節奏感。具速度感的線條流暢地在空
間中流轉，進行造形美感的探討。一套17件可以任意組合。

文殊五字咒 Manjusri 5-word Sutra

2005, 3 X 3 X 8 cm, 7 pcs
青田石Stone，共7件

大慈大悲咒

Infinitely Merciful and Great Compassion Sutra

2005, 2.4 X 2.4 X 7 cm, 9 pcs
長白山石 Stone，共29件

百字明

Vajra Hundred words Sutra (The hundred syllable mantra)

2005, 6 X 6 X 6 cm, 5 pcs

青田石 Stone，共5件

詠 Chant

2006, 17 X 14.5 X 21.5 cm

蕭山石Stone

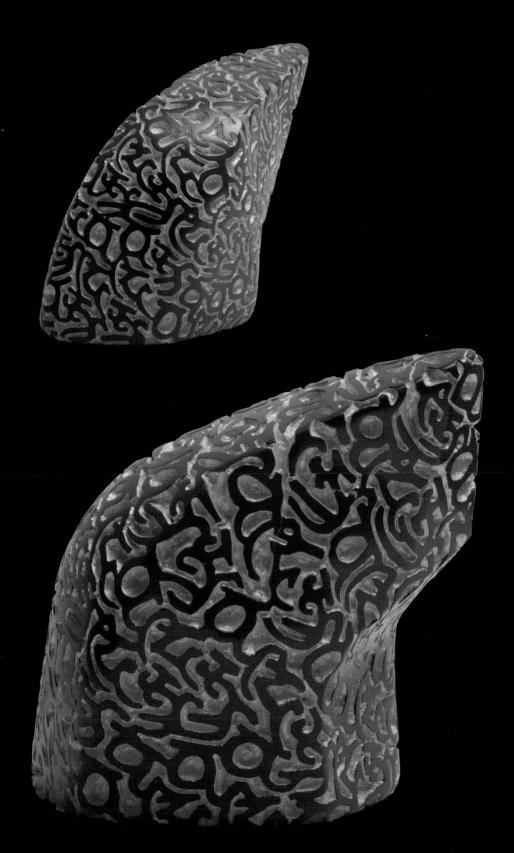

詠 Chant

2006, 17 X 14.5 X 21.5 cm

蕭山石Stone

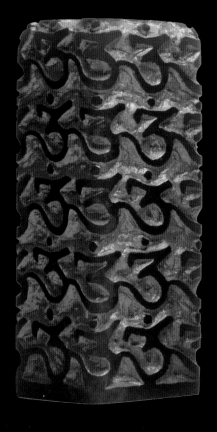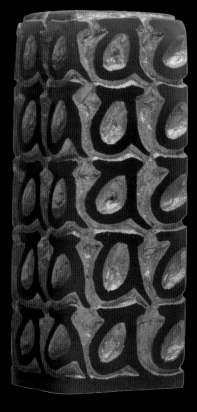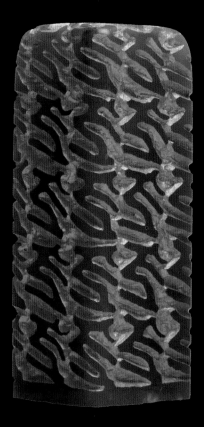

大慈大悲咒心咒

Spell of heart of Infinitely Merciful and Great Compassion Sutra

2006, 5.2 X 5.2 X 14 cm, 6 pcs

遼東石 Stone，共6件

以重複的悉曇文佈滿作品表面，運用篆刻「以朱計白，以白計朱」的美學慨念，創作虛實相應的書法刻石。

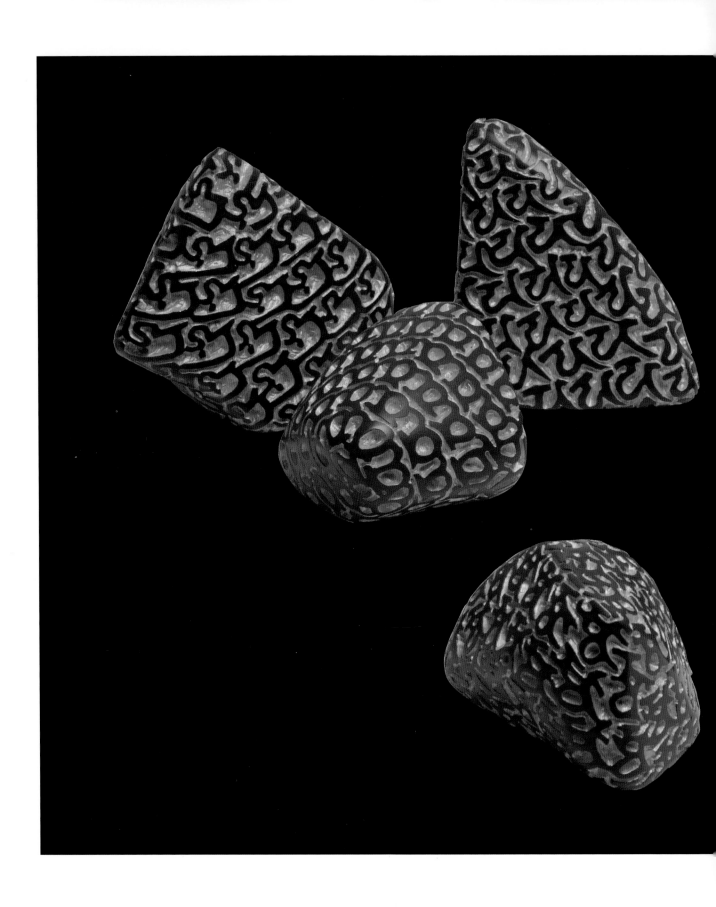

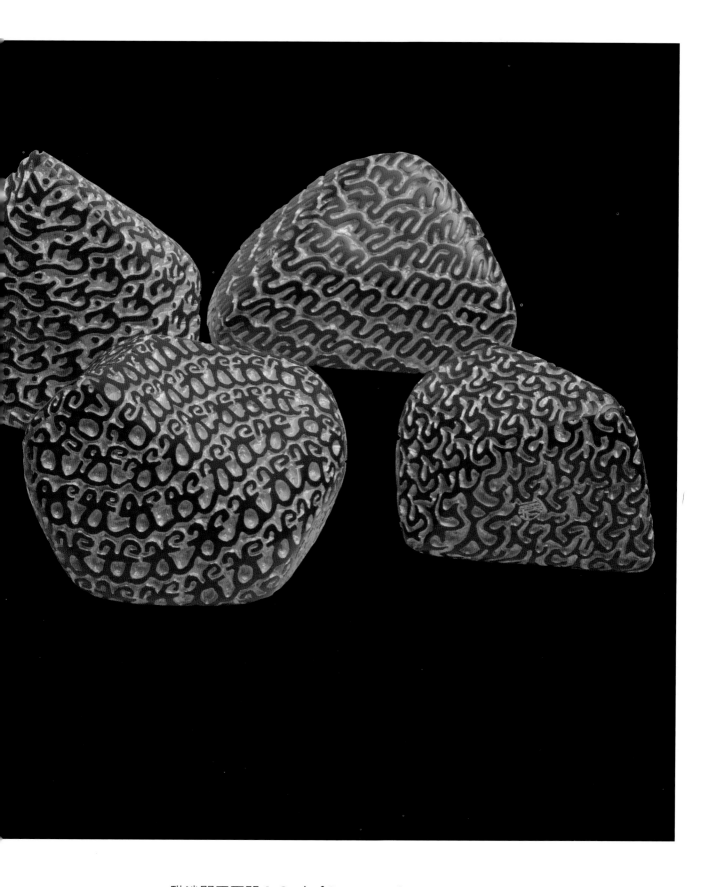

毗沙門天王咒-1 God of Prosperity Sutra

2006, 8 pcs
蕭山石 Stone，共8件

以悉曇文創作的「文字皴」系列作品。重複的悉曇文佈滿山形石表面，交織成
虛實相應、緊疏相乘的「文字皴」傳達山水畫的美學概念，組構立體的抽象山
水，並結合日本「枯山水」造園概念，將八件刻石作品任意組合，創造不同的
群山景象。

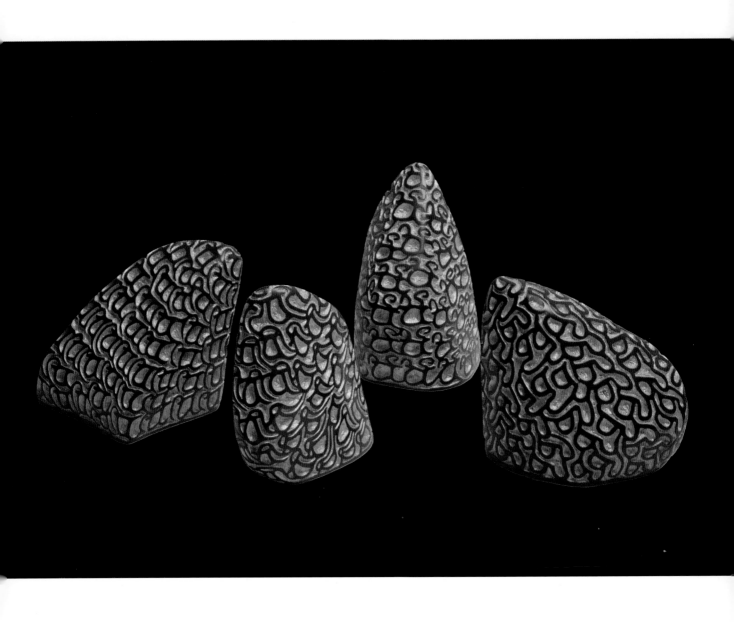

佛法四大天王

Four Heavenly Kings(Caturmaharajakayikas)

2006, 4 pcs
蕭山石 Stone，共4件

以佛教四大天王（或稱四大金剛）為母題所創作的「文字皴系列」作品。中國的佛教徒認為南方增長天王，代表「風」；東方持國天王，代表「調」；北方多聞天王，代表「雨」；西方廣目天天王，代表「順」。組合起來便是「風調雨順」。

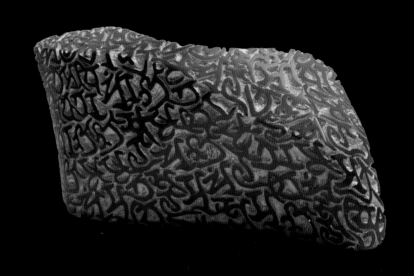

以重複的悉曇文佈滿作品表面，交織成虛實相應、緊疏相乘
的「文字皴」將中國山水畫體現於刻石之中。

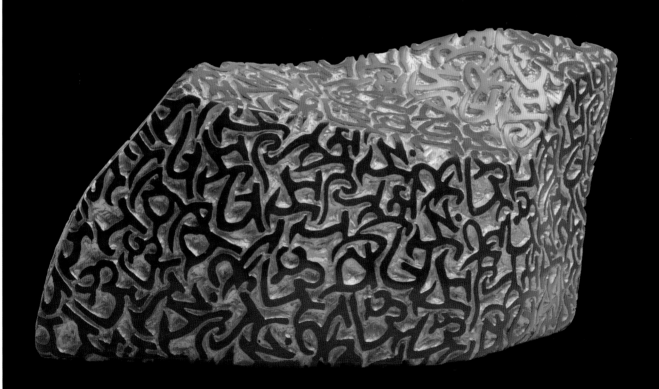

璀璨 Resplendent

2006, 45.8 X 16.5 X 23.5 cm

蕭山石 Stone

以重複的悉曇文佈滿作品表面，交織成虛實相應、緊疏相乘
的「文字皴」將中國山水畫體現於刻石之中。

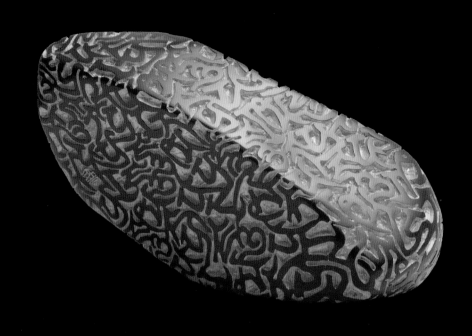

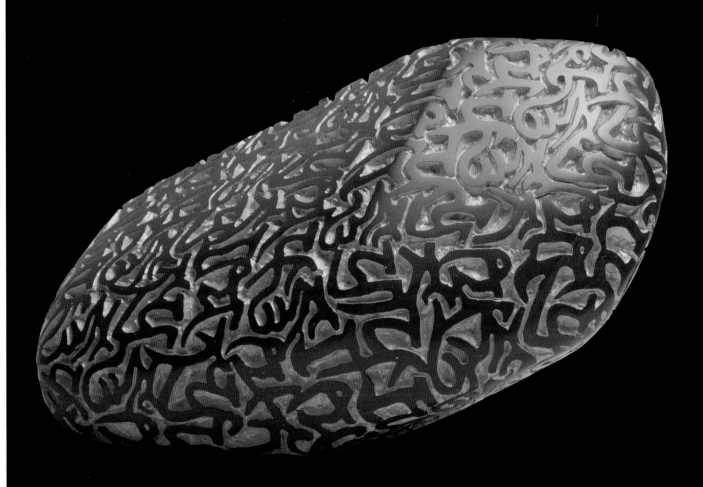

般若波羅密多 Perfection of Wisdom

2006, 34.5 X 19 X 21.5 cm

蕭山石 Stone

般若波羅密多爲梵語的音譯
般若，原意爲通達「妙智慧」
波羅，指「到彼岸」，有解脫罣礙之意。
密多，意思是「無極」

整句話的意思爲「透過心量廣大的通達智慧，超脫世
俗的困苦。」

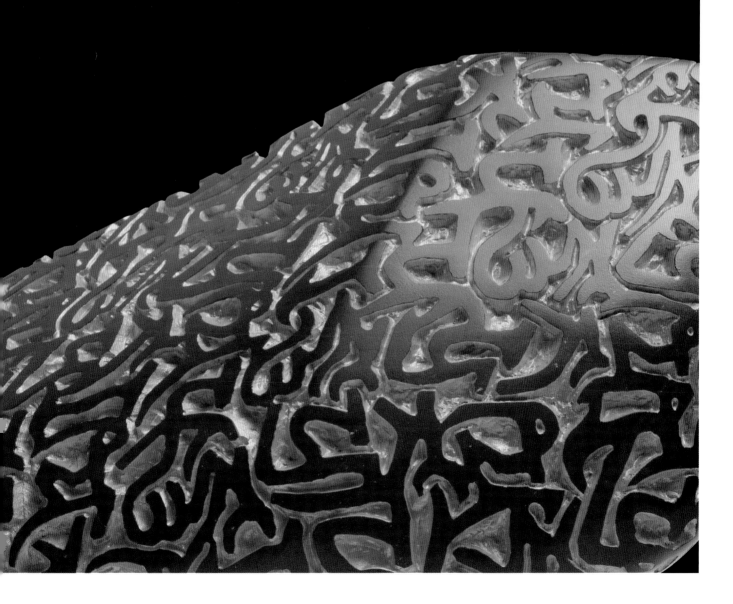

菩提 Bodhi

2006, 39.2 X 20 X 20.5 cm

蕭山石　Stone

菩提是悉曇文Bodhi的音譯，意思是指「不昧生死輪迴，導致涅盤的覺悟。」修證菩提是佛教徒最崇高的理念。

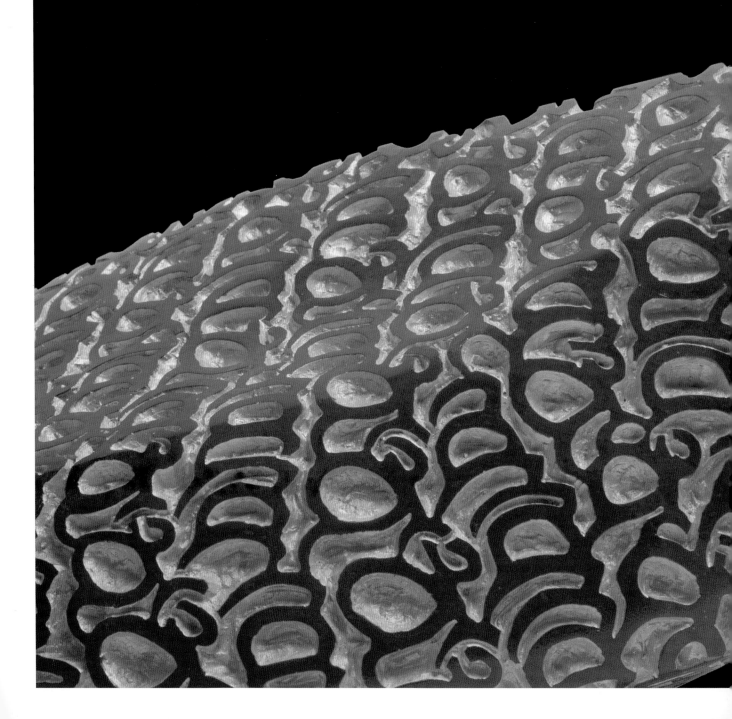

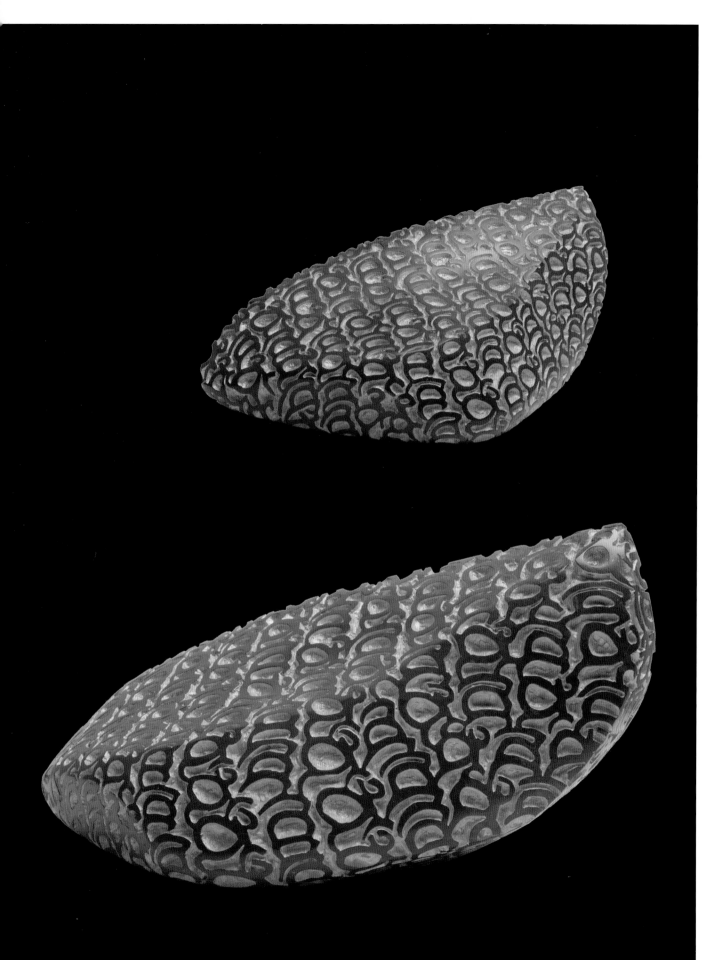

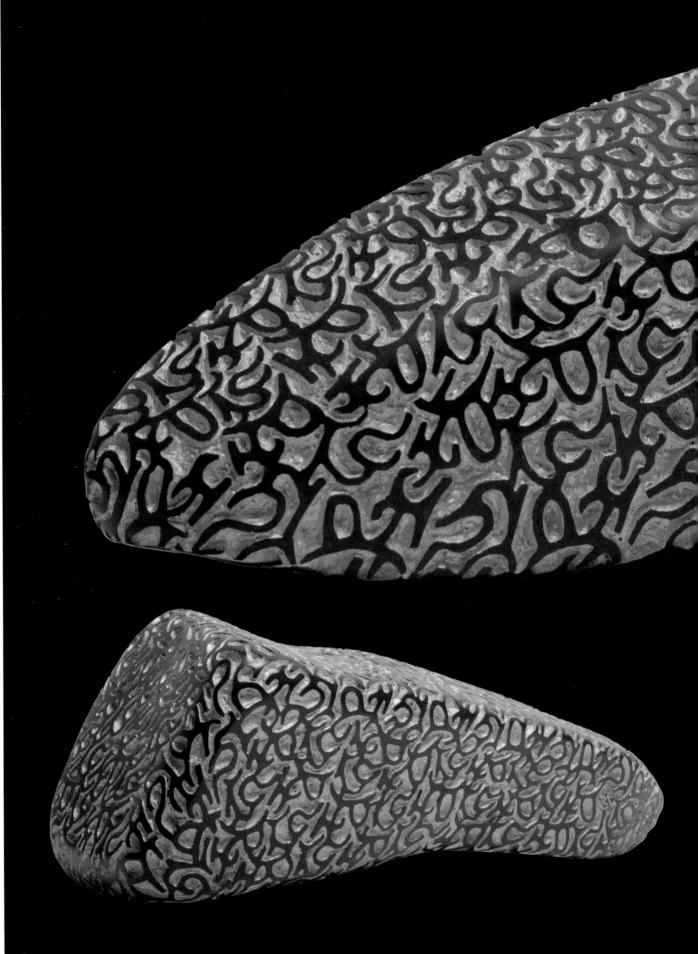

將悉曇字當作「繪畫元素」不斷重複，傳達作者自身的情緒與情感。如同作曲者以音符組成樂句，再把樂句組合成樂章一般。這種類似「音樂感通」的創作歷程，是由佛教誦經、音樂以及冥想得到的發想。

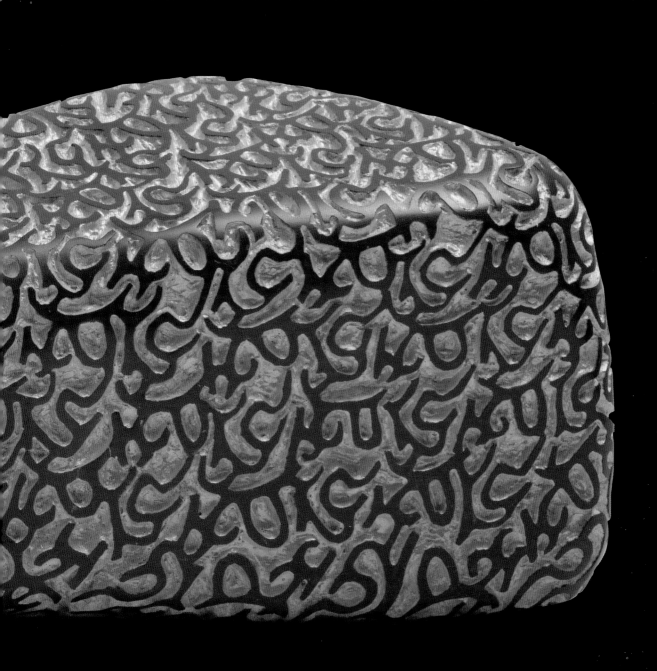

娑婆訶 Svaha

2007, 42.5 X 15 X 17.5 cm
蕭山石 Stone

將悉曇字當作「繪畫元素」不斷重複，傳達作者自身的情緒與情感。如同作曲者以音符組成樂句，再把樂句組合成樂章一般。這種類似「音樂感通」的創作歷程，是由佛教誦經、音樂以及冥想得到的發想。

娑波訶為結尾文，通常置於佛教咒語最後，意思為「成就」、「吉祥」、「圓滿」。

觀自在 Avalokitesvara(GuanYin)

2007, 40.5 X 12 X 22.5 cm, 32 X 18 X 16.8 cm

蕭山石 Stone

「觀自在」是觀音菩薩的另一個稱號，觀音菩薩無論是自利或利人
都能得到大自在。我們能觀照自己、認識自己，就能自在了；我
們關照他人能夠「人我不二」又怎會不自在？

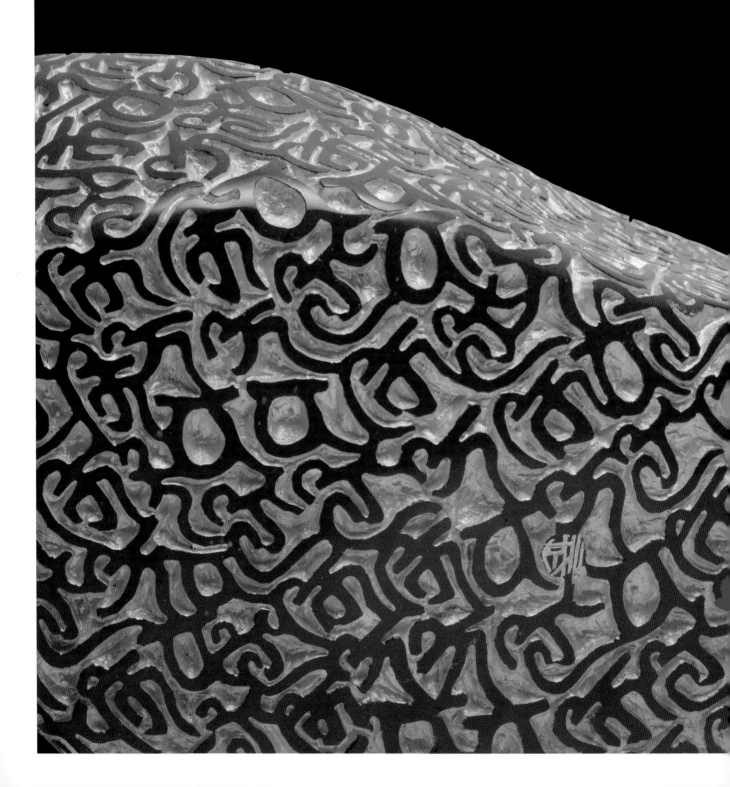

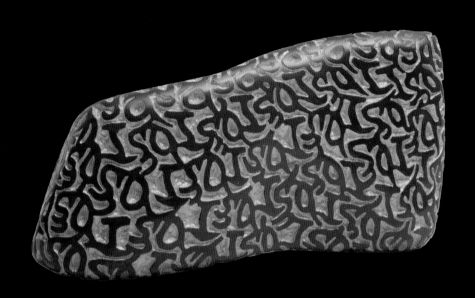
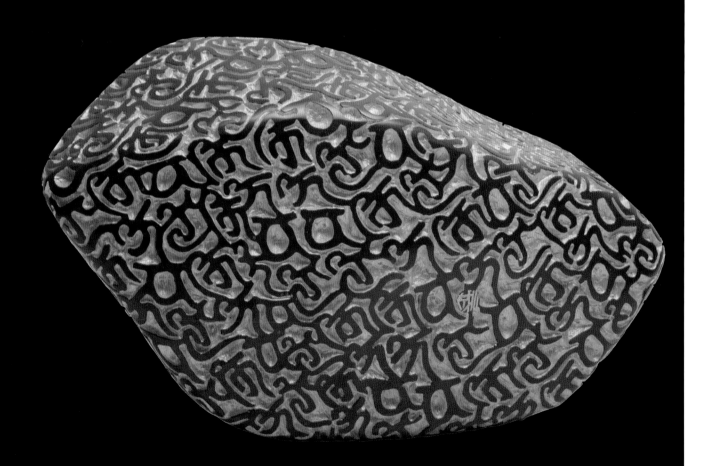

讚 Praise

2007, 22.5 X 15.8 X 26.5 cm

蕭山石 Stone

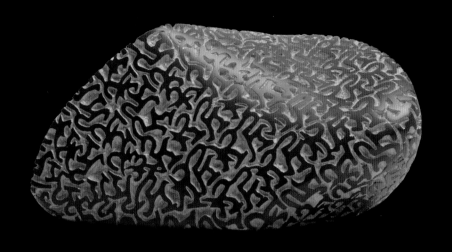

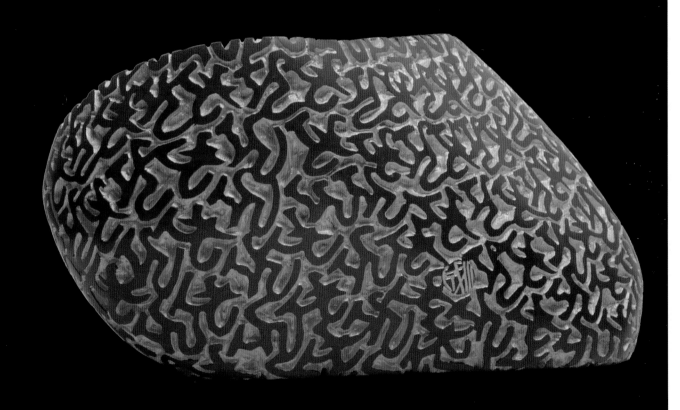

美 Beauty

2007, 31 X 15 X 16.3 cm

蕭山石 Stone

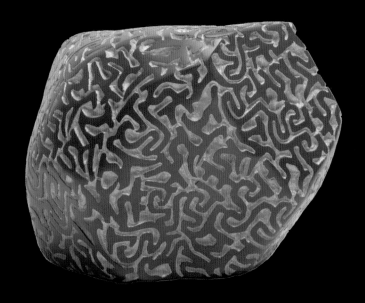

吉 Auspicious

2007, 21 X 16.5 X 16.3 cm

蕭山石 Stone

2007, 44.5 X 12 X 19.5 cm
蕭山石 Stone

「悉曇」一詞，與梵字或梵語相同，本意
「成就」，是互證的圓滿，也是自證的成就。

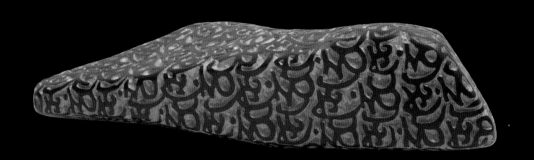

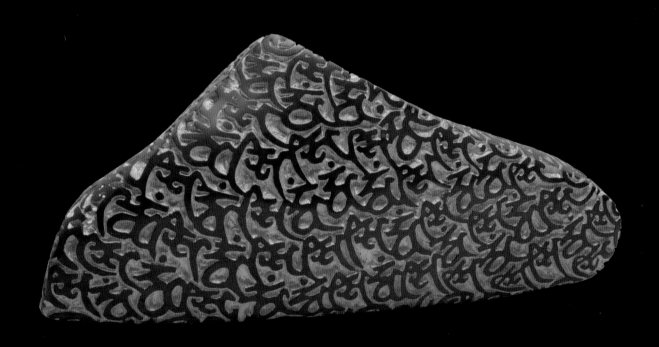

悉曇 Siddham

2007, 44.5 X 12 X 19.5 cm
蕭山石 Stone

「悉曇」一詞，與梵字或梵語相同，本意
「成就」，是互證的圓滿，也是自證的成就。

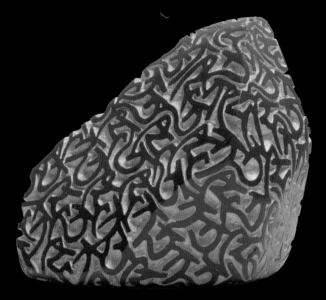

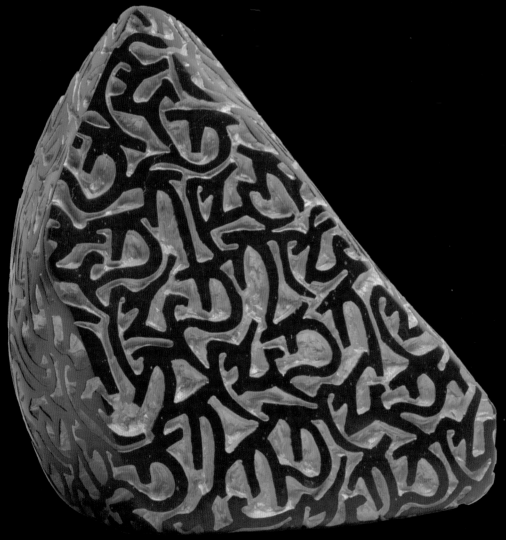

興 Prosperous

2007, 23 X 19.5 X 22.5 cm

蕭山石　Stone

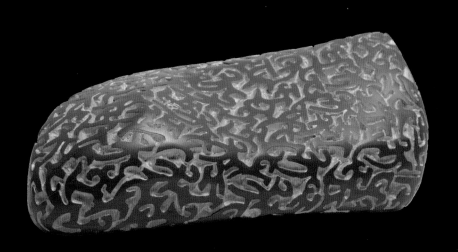

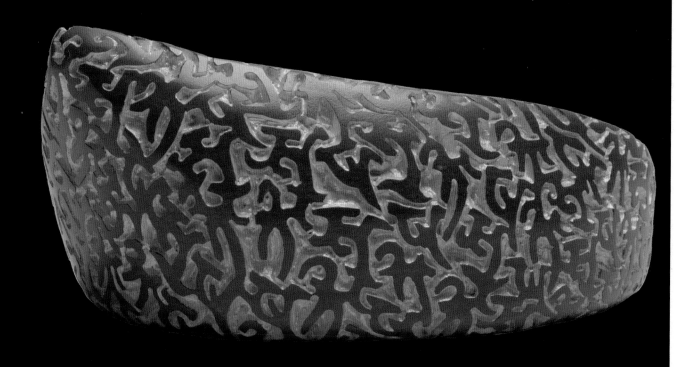

歡樂 Joyous

2007 ,24 X 13.2 X 10.8 cm

蕭山石 Stone

升 Ascend

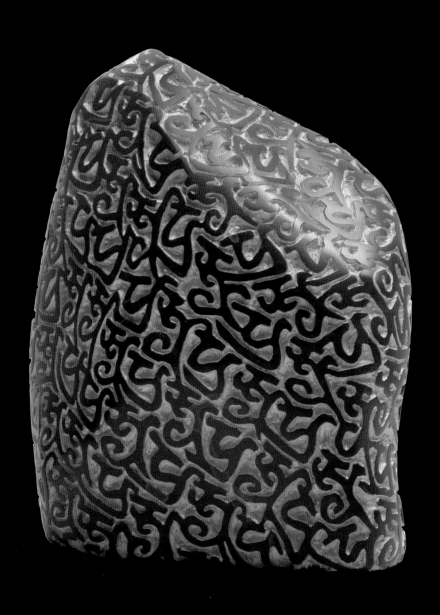

升 Ascend

2008, 25 X 16.5 X 31 cm

蕭山石 Stone

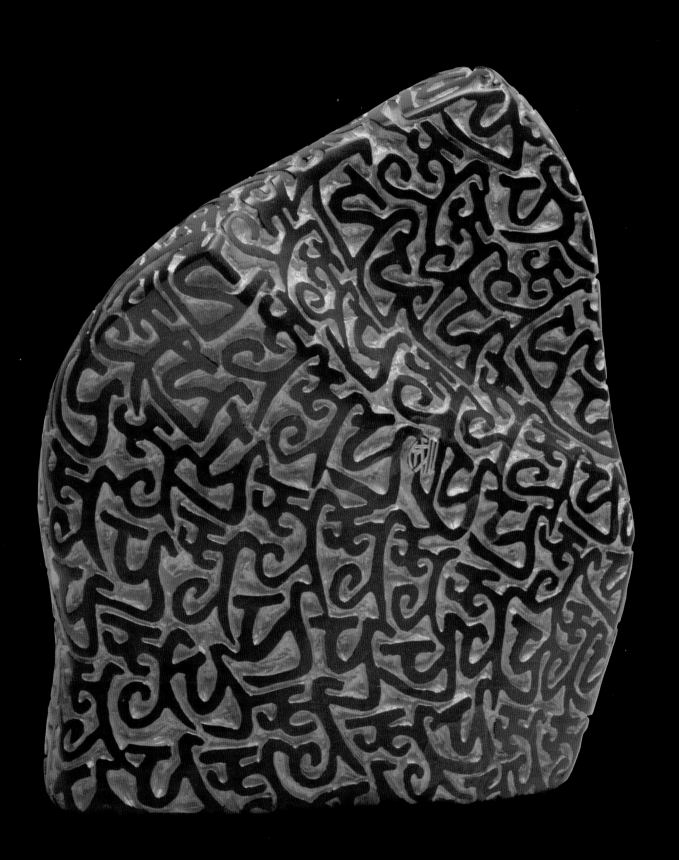

喜 Delighted

2008, 22 X 14 X 17.6 cm

蕭山石 Stone

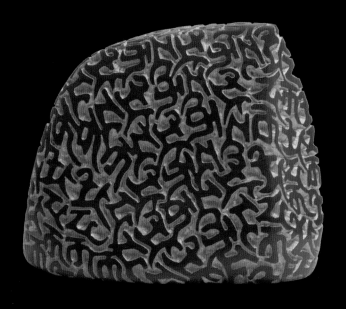

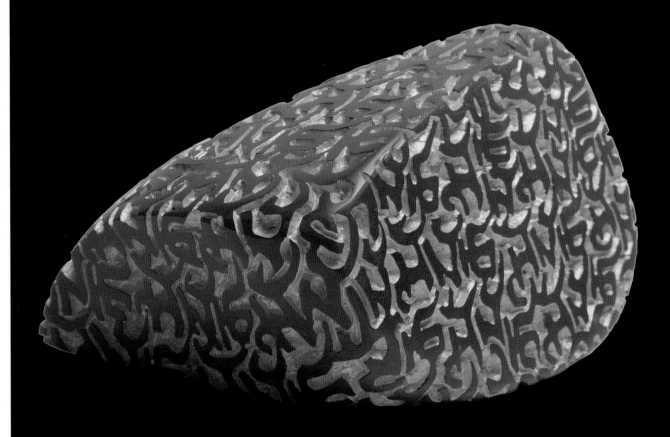

喜 Delighted

2008, 22 X 14 X 17.6 cm

蕭山石 Stone

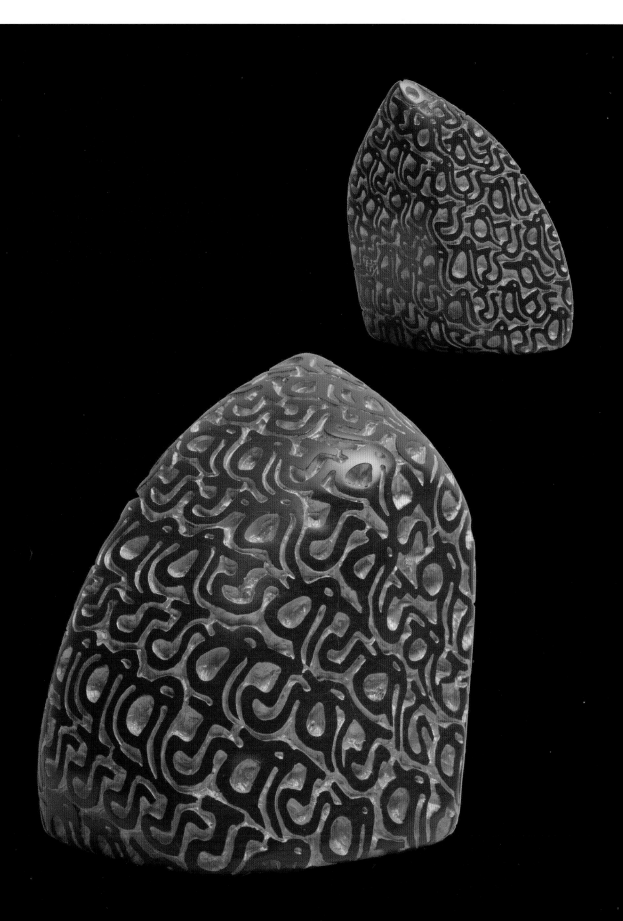

精進 Superior

2008, 18.5 X 14 X 20.3 cm

蕭山石 Stone

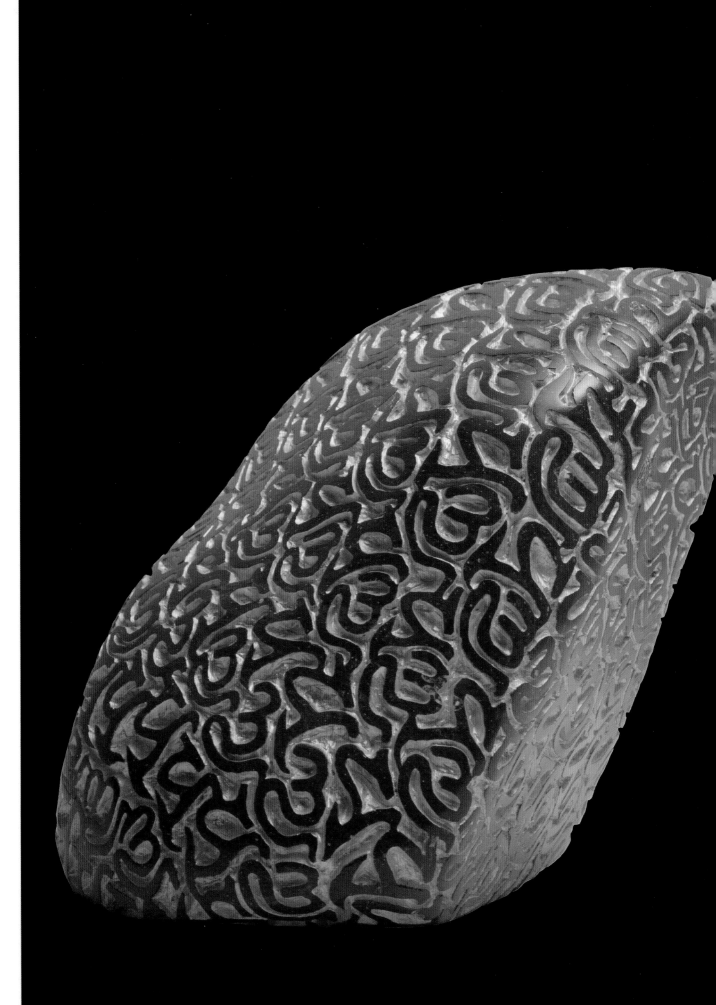

福 Fortunate

2008, 30.5 X 23 X 26.5 cm

蕭山石 Stone

將一個個文字當作有生命的「細胞」，組
構出新形式的雕塑。

福 Fortunate

2008, 30.5 X 23 X 26.5 cm
蕭山石 Stone

將一個個文字當作有生命的「細胞」，組
構出新形式的雕塑。

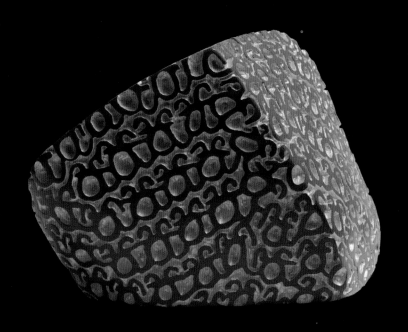

種子字的梵文為bija，本意是植物的種子。佛、菩薩以及天
王，通常取其梵文名稱或咒語的第一字或者是最重要的一字
作為種子字，用來代表本尊。

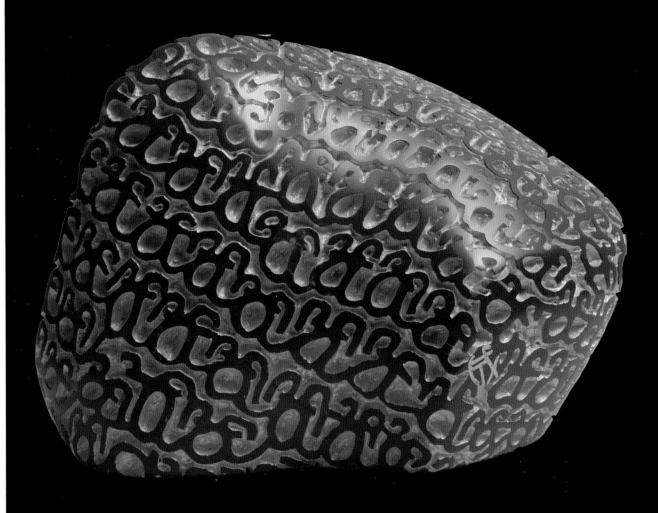

毗沙門天王種子字 Vessavana Hri (Seed words)

2008, 27 X 17.5 X 18cm

蕭山石 Stone

種子字的梵文為bija，本意是植物的種子。佛、菩薩以及天
王，通常取其梵文名稱或咒語的第一字或者是最重要的一字
作為種子字，用來代表本尊。

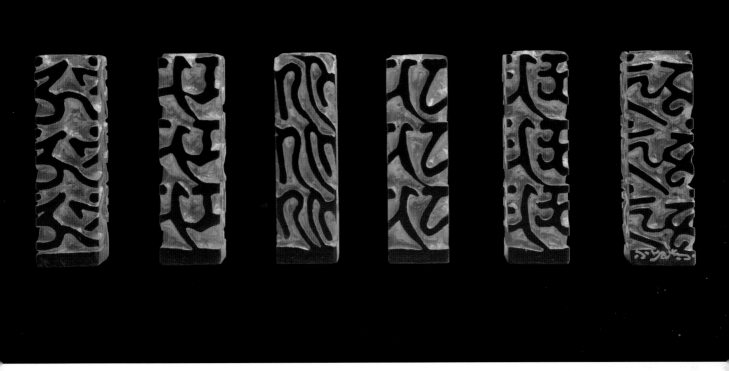

六字大明咒

Om Mani Padme Hum (The Six Syllabled Mantra)

2008, 3 X 3 X 10 cm, 6pcs

天山紫石 Stone，共6件

六字大明咒又名六字眞言，是佛教裡最常見的眞言（mantra），是觀世音菩薩願力與加持的結晶，又稱爲觀世音的心咒。漢音譯爲「唵嘛呢叭咪吽」按照梵文字面解釋爲：「向持有珍寶蓮花的聖者敬禮祈請，摧破煩惱。」

毗沙門天王咒心咒-2 God of Prosperity Sutra-2

2008, 51 X 18 X 23.5 cm

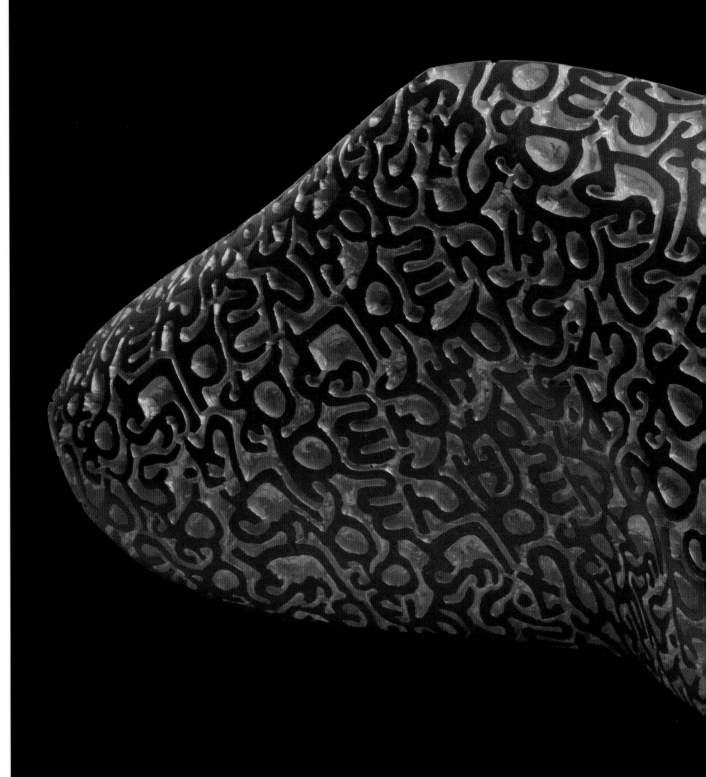

毗沙門天王咒心咒-2 God of Prosperity
Sutra-2

2008, 51 X 18 X 23.5 cm

蕭山石 Stone

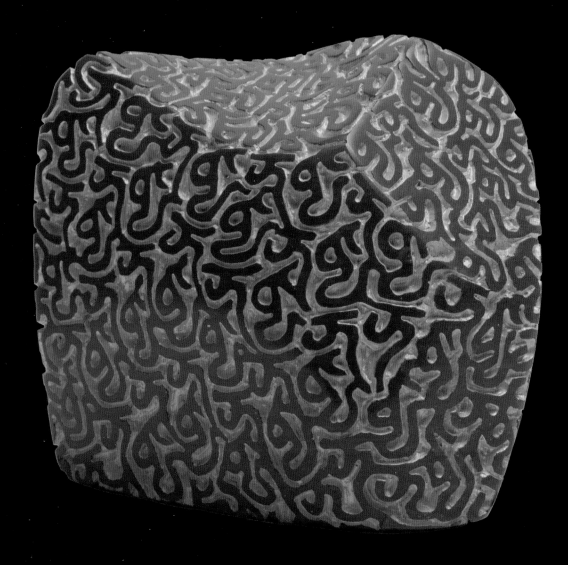

禪 Zen

2007, 20 X 14 X 17.5 cm

蕭山石 Stone

漢字刻石

Sculpture
of Chinese Calligraphy

道德經 Daoist Classic(Laozi)

1992-1994, 15 X 15 X 30 cm, 12pcs
巴林石 Stone，共12件

李鎮成創作這件作品的整體性架構是以12件石材代表中國的十二地支為主軸，若仔細觀察，第一件頂部以內方外圓，作為形容剛正、圓融處事態度；而「老子」二字採取內陰，「道德經」三字則以外陽方式呈現。象徵陰陽調合，屬宇宙天體運轉自然平衡之法則，其整體是以「道法自然」為最高原則。「道德經」使用渾厚自然的商周金文、大籀為主。其內文如有相同字出現皆以不同寫法表現。

「道德經」亦延續了將文字作為視覺符號的創作理念，將原本篆刻處理印面的觀念轉換為有機的構成，李鎮成更靈活地運用石材的整體，並以組合式的構成，可以隨意安排這組作品的形式，經過隨意更動組合形式之後，「道德經」與李鎮成另一件同樣出自古代經典的石刻作品「離騷」一樣，出現了捨棄文字的意涵；僅有按照道德經最初的敘述順序安排，這件作品才能表示主題內容的表述思想意義。如果依照場地、呈現方式等條件的不同將作品作隨機組合，則不再是按照老子思想去解讀的範圍了。

在頗長的一段平面性線條的思考之後，李鎮成的創作，逐漸隔開文字本身所具含的表意概念，將文字當作結構性的有機組成，並透過意象化完成中國文字多重的可能。事實上，中國文字表意的概念，是一般觀賞者面對作品時最大的阻礙。觀賞者若執著於文字的實用意義，便無法進入作者的文字美學領域。李鎮成現階段的作品將平面文字立體化，把需要依靠載體支撐的線條，具體地以立體的觀念呈現。因此，李鎮成的擺脫文字依附於平面的圍限之後，作品更加自由，更具有開闊的想像空間，對創作語言和符號的運用，也逐漸純粹起來。

摘錄自胡懿勳：《道德經刻石簡介》

苦熱 Heat

1989, 20.8 X 12.3 X 26 cm

泰來石 Stone

「苦熱」是李鎮成第一件「文字皴」系列雕塑作品。當時他以篆書佈滿山形的泰
來石表面，可以看出他試圖將文字單純地作為一種視覺符號的表象。

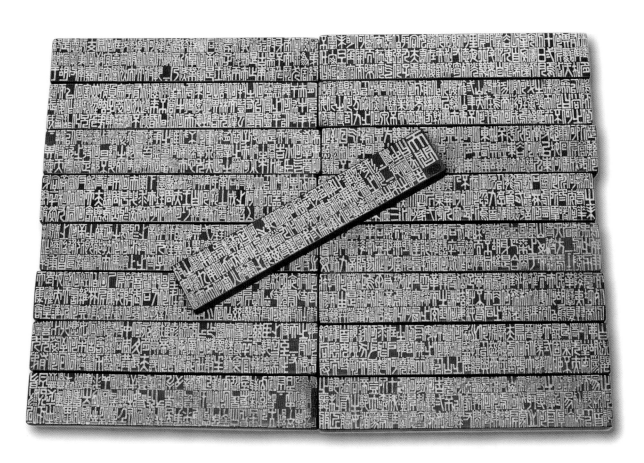

天問 Verse on the Heaven

1988, 21.8 X 3.8 X 1.3 cm, 17 pcs
端石 Stone，共17件

以十七件端石創作的《天問》，可按照不同的展示需要轉換組合形式，打破文字
內容的順序，將文字單純的作為視覺符號，讓文字超越實用性的表象功能。

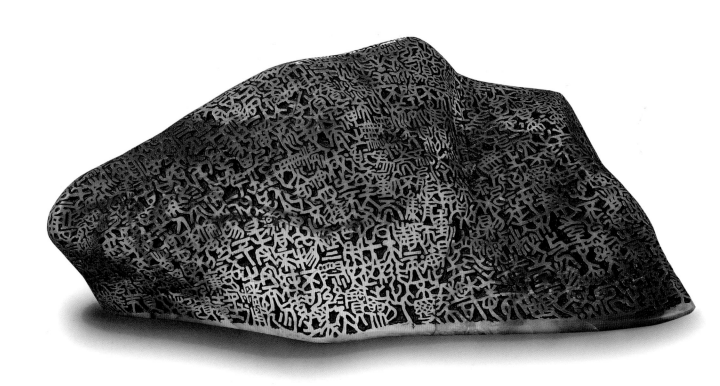

刻意 Intention

1990, 45.7 X 23.3 X 16.5 cm
巴林石 Stone

利用石材本身的色澤、文理和造形，以書法線條結合而成的文字皴，表現山石
陰陽、虛實的質感與肌理。

參同契 Poem

1991, 13.1 X 13.8 X 30.5 cm
巴林石 Stone

將禪宗大師石頭希遷的禪詩作品《參同契》刻在方形石頭表面，充分表現篆書
的美感。

春江花月夜 The Spring River in the Moon Nigtht

1990, 31.5 X 19.8 X 14.0 cm

巴林雞血石 Stone

清夜無塵月色如銀 Silent Night and Bright Moon

2000, 16.5 X 18.6 X 19.8 cm , 15.5 X 13.8 X 18.6 cm
巴林石 Stone，共2件

漁翁 Fisherman

1991, 12.0 X 6.2 X 11.7 cm

青田石 Stone

二十四詩品 Twenty-four Poems

1989，巴林石 Stone，共24件

千年石 Ancient Stone

2001， 23.2 X 13.5 X 16.5 cm

江西石 Stone

千字文
Thousand Character Classic

2003～2007, 2.4 X 2.4 X 7 cm, 1000 pcs
峨嵋石Stone，共1000件

千字文相傳是公元六世紀初梁武帝命員外散騎侍郎周興嗣依王羲之書跡一千字不重複者編綴而成；據說周興嗣一天便完成了。原名為《次韻王羲之書千字》，後世簡稱為《千字文》。又有另一種說法是三國魏太守鍾繇所書，而王羲之再加以改寫者。

千字文極受歷代書法家的重視並屢為傳寫。主要是因為這一千個單字幾乎涵蓋了最常用的漢字之半，而在漢文字的發展歷程上，這些字基本都已定型。更重要的是其造型結體係根據王羲之的書法而來，具備各種審美元素，不僅是學習認字的啟蒙教材，也是研習書法乃至從事書道創作的不竭泉源。據說智永生平便寫了各體千字文八百通分送江南各寺院，作為有志學書者的範本，可見以千字文為書法研習或創作指南自始即是中國書法界有意識的發明，也是所有從事書道藝術創作者必修的傳統藝程。

李鎮成的《千字文》刻石作品，將一千個字分別刻為造型單元，每個造型單元皆由一個字組成。這一千個造型單元可以任意組合，一個、兩個、三個、四個、五個，乃至百個、千個。而每一種組合都可以產生不同的意義；若不加以組合，則每一個單元本身就是一個字，它的意義也是多重的。這裡透露著漢字最關緊要的一個特質，即每個漢字本身都是多義的；把幾個漢字組合在一起便產生許多不同的詞意或句意。將一千個造型單元組合在一起，形成壯觀的文字景觀，與文字皺系列作品，有異曲同工之妙。

山居八詠 Live in Mountains

2004, 7.8 X 7.8 X 9 cm, 8 Pieces
巴林石 Stone，共8件

將草書線條佈滿長方體作品表面，運用篆刻「以朱計白，以白計朱」的美學概念，創作虛實相應的書法刻石。

無題 Untitled

2004, 3 X 3 X 7 cm, 8 Pieces
奉天凍石 Stone，共8件

和泥合水 Knead

1996, 15 X 15 X 30 cm
巴林石 Stone

清夜 Silent Night

1996, 15 X 15 X 30 cm
巴林石 Stone

清風皓月 Bright Moon with a Breeze

1998, 15 X 15 X 30 cm

巴林石 Stone

磊磊 Heap of Stone

1999, 15 X 15 X 30 cm

巴林石 Stone

為樂 Making Fun

1997, 5.5 X 5.8 X 15 cm

蕭山石 Stone

證悟 Awake to Truth

1998, 15 X 15 X 30 cm

巴林石 Stone

丹青 Painting

1998, 9 X 9 X 9 cm
巴林石 Stone

千山 A Thousand Mountain

1998, 12 X 11.6 X 8.5 cm
巴林石 Stone

母子 Mother and Son

1998, 22 X 10.5 X 14.5 cm
巴林石 Stone

證果 Testify achievements

1990, 12 X 2 X 9.3 cm
泰來石 Stone

偶來松樹下 A Leisurely Free from Restraint

1995, 19.5 X 2.7 X 5.4 cm
江西石 Stone

自在 Unrestricted

1997, 9 X 9 X 9 cm

巴林石 Stone

苦寒吟 Chant of Coldness

1990, 10.8 X 8.6 X 9.2 cm

泰來石 Stone

春宵自遣 Self release at spring night

1991, 11.5 X 4.5 X 13 cm

青田石 Stone

夢井 Well of Dreams

1990, 9 X 16 X 10 cm

巴林石 Stone

雪晴晚望 Night without Snowing

1991, 11 X 5 X 11.5 cm

青田石 Stone

行雲 Moving Clouds

1990, 12 X 2 X 9.3 cm

泰來石 Stone

園,Garden

1991, 9.6 X 6.5 X 15 cm

青田石 Stone

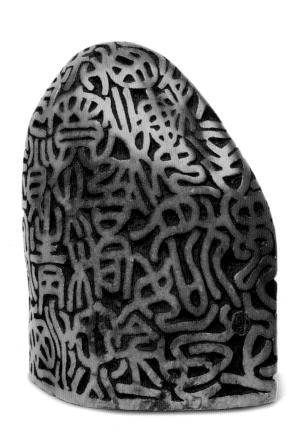

相見歡 Joy at Meeting

1991, 12.9 X 6.2 X 16.8 cm

青田石 Stone

遊溪 Play in the stream

1991, 16.5 X 6.5X 17.5 cm

青田石 Stone

處士盧岕山居 Visiting a Friend

1991, 11.5 X 7.0 X 17.7 cm

巴林石 Stone

題秋江獨釣圖 Go Fishing Alone

1994, 3 X 3 X 9.5 cm
巴林石 Stone

醉眠 Get Drunk

1995, 3 X 3 X 7 cm
巴林石 Stone

一川雲 A Cloud River

6 X 6 X 9 cm
巴林石 Stone

書呰呰且休休 Stop working to relax

1994, 3 X 3 X 9.5 cm

巴林石 Stone

松老雲閒曠然自適
An old pine tree and idle cloud
with free atmosphere

1991, 4 X 5 X 7.5 cm

巴林石 Stone

林間鳥弄春音
Birds singing in the woods in Spring

1991, 5 X 5 X 8 cm

青田石 Stone

白露橫江水光接天
White dew covers river and river reflects the sky

2005, 4.3 X 4 X 10.5 cm
巴林石 Stone

無邊 Borderless

2005, 6 X 6 X 10.5 cm
泰來石 Stone

鼓吹 Urge

2004, 8 X 8 X 8 cm
青田石　Stone

竹敲風弄菊
The Wind Makes Bamboo
and Chrysanthemum tapping

2004, 7.7 X 7.7 X 9 cm
巴林石 Stone

江山清趣
The delight of landscape

2005, 4 X 4 X 12 cm
遼東石 Stone

細草微風岸
A light wind is rippling
at the grassy shore

2004, 8.7 X 8.7 X 9 cm
巴林石　Stone

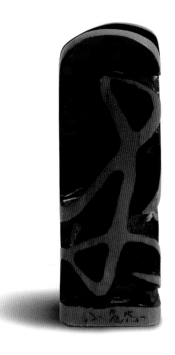

天樂 Heaven Music

2005, 4.5 X 4.5 X 13 cm

峨嵋石 Stone

鴻飛冥冥青楓葉赤
The wild goose flies to the unseen world,
the green leaves of maple trees turns to red.

2005, 4.5 X 4.5 X 14.5 cm

峨嵋石 Stone

清川 A Clear Stream

2000, 6 X 6 X 11 cm

泰來石 Stone

雲水之蹤無住無心
The tracks of cloud and water
are non-stop and unwitting

2005, 4.5 X 4.5 X 14.5 cm
峨嵋石 Stone

青春恰自來 Youth comes by itself

2004, 8.5 X 9 X 9 cm
巴林石 Stone

一花一世界 A flower is a world

2004, 8.7 X 8.7 X 9 cm
巴林石 Stone

悟道聞聲
Realize the truth by hearing the voice

2005, 4.5 X 4.5 X 6.5 cm
遼東石 Stone

月到天心
Moon in the middle of the sky

2006, 3.8 X 3.8 X 7 cm
壽山石 Stone

雲來巫峽長月出雪山白
Clouds make Wu-Gorge looks longer,
moonlight brighten the Snow Mountain

2004, 8.2 X 8.2 X 9 cm
巴林石 Stone

青山不語 Silent mountains

2005, 5.2 X 4 X 7 cm

巴林石 Stone

天清月澄 Clear sky with bright moon

2004, 9.5 X 9.5 X 10 cm

青田石 Stone

墨舞 Dancing writing

2005, 4.5 X 4.5 X 7 cm

壽山石 Stone

簾外薰風燕語
Warm breeze with soft chirping
of swallow outside the screen

2005, 11.2 X 5 X 9 cm
青田石 Stone

風細飛花相逐 Petals flying with wind

2006, 5.8 X 5.8 X 8 cm
巴林石 Stone

一灣水綠繞屋
A clear stream around the house

2005, 4.5 X 4.5 X 8 cm
巴林石 Stone

行雲流水
Floating clouds and flowing water

2005, 4.3 X 4.3 X 8 cm
巴林石　Stone

煙霏霧淞
Flying snow and rain rimes the scene

2005, 4.5 X 4.5 X 9 cm
泰來石　Stone

和風清穆
Breeze makes the air clean

2005, 4.5 X 4.5 X 8 cm
巴林石　Stone

星皎月潔
Bright stars and moon

2005, 4 X 4 X 9 cm
泰來石 Stone

茶甌日泛雲腴
Steam curling up around the tea cup

2005, 6 X 6 X 6 cm
青田石 Stone

微風閑坐古松
Sitting under the old pine with breeze

2005, 5.6 X 5.6 X 8 cm
巴林 Stone

清江近月
Clear river with moon reflection

2005, 3 X 3 X 10 cm
遼東石 Stone

珠雪玉霜
snow round as pearl and frost pure as jade

2005, 4.3 X 4.3 X 8 cm
巴林石 Stone

臨野水看浮雲
Appreciate floating clouds at the river bank

2006, 5.8 X 5.8 X 6.8 cm
遼東石 Stone

花明麗月鳥口弄芳園
Birds visit the garden with beautiful flowers
under bright moonlight

2005, 6 X 6 X 7 cm
遼東石 Stone

風急天高渚清沙白
Fast wind blows sand high
to the air and clean the ground

2005, 4.5 X 4.5 X 8 cm
巴林石 Stone

仰觀山俯聽泉
Face upward to observe mountains,
bow to listen water flowing

2005, 6 X 6 X 6 cm
青田石 Stone

竹松挺秀
Tall and graceful bamboos and pines

2006, 3.2 X 3.2 X 10 cm
遼東石 Stone

氣調四序風和萬籟
Timely seasons with wonderful weather

2006, 5.8 X 5.8 X 6.8 cm
遼東石 Stone

濯清泉以自潔
Rinse with clear water to clean

2005, 6.4 X 6.5 X 8 cm
巴林石 Stone

碧草 Green grass

2006, 2.3 X 2.3 X 7 cm
巴林石 Stone

清泉 Clean Springs

2006, 2 X 2 X 6.5 cm
巴林石 Stone

長樂無極 Endless Happiness

2006, 7.8 X 3 X 6.3 cm
巴林石 Stone

竹情花意
Affection of bamboos
and intention of flowers

2005, 8 X 2.6 X 5.5 cm
巴林石 Stone

一頂斗笠藏世界
A bamboo hat covers the world

2005, 8.5 X 4.5 X 9 cm
青田石 Stone

溪路夕陽芳草
Green grass along the stream at the sunset

2005, 5.3 X 3.4 X 6.7 cm
巴林石 Stone

黑雲翻墨 Dancing writing

2005, 4.5 X 4.5 X 7 cm

壽山石 Stone

白露橫江水光接天

White dew covers river and river reflects the sky

2005, 8.5 X 3.2 X 7 cm

巴林石 Stone

一頂斗笠藏世界

A bamboo Hat Covers the World

2005, 7.8 X 3.8 X 5.6 cm

巴林石 Stone

月入懷 Moon In the Arms

2005, 4 X 4 X 8 cm
青田石 Stone

竹露 Dew on Bamboo

2005, 3.5 X 3.5 X 7.5 cm
青田石 Stone

自然法爾
It's what it is by nature

2005, 3.3 X 3.3 X 7.5 cm
青田石 Stone

如是我聞
What I heard is the truth

2005, 3.8 X 3.8 X 8 cm
青田石 Stone

荷風 Wind with lotus smell

2005, 3 X 3 X 7.5 cm
巴林石 Stone

菩提 Bodhi

2005, 3 X 3 X 9 cm
遼東石 Stone

說文解字刻石
Sculpture
of Six Writings

此系列作品是根據漢字的六種構造形式——象形、指示、形聲、會意、轉注、假借等，所創作的立體文字。

六書是東漢許慎、鄭眾、班固等人根據漢字的形成所作的整理，並非漢字的造字法則。六書一詞最早出現於《周禮》：「保氏掌諫王惡，而養國子以道，乃教之六藝：一曰五禮；二曰六樂；三曰五射；四曰五馭；五曰六書；六曰九數；」。《周禮》只記述了「六書」這個名詞，卻未加以說明。因此《周禮》中提到的「六書」可能與今日之概念截然不同。

東漢學者許慎在《說文解字》說到：「周禮八歲入小學，保氏教國子，先以六書。一曰指事：指事者，視而可識，察而可見，「上」、「下」是也。二曰象形：象形者，畫成其物，隨體詰詘，「日」、「月」是也。三曰形聲：形聲者，以事為名，取譬相成，「江」、「河」是也。四曰會意：會意者，比類合誼，以見指撝，「武」、「信」是也。五曰轉註：轉註者，建類一首，同意相受，「考」、「老」是也。六曰假借：假借者，本無其字，依聲托事，「令」、「長」是也。」這是歷史上首次正式對六書定義。目前一般對六書的解說以許慎為主。

回 Return(hui)

1999, 16.5 X 14 X 26 cm

蕭山石 Stone

千山 A Thousand Mountain

1999, 24 X 16 X 29.5 cm

蕭山石 Stone

仲 In the Middle

2000, 20 X 14 X 20 cm
蕭山石 Stone

位 Position(wei)

2000, 36 X 19 X 25 cm
蕭山石 Stone

問 Ask(wen)

2000, 23 X 16 X 28 cm

蕭山石 Stone

人人-1 Two People-1

2001, 23.8 X 15.5 X 22 cm

蕭山石 Stone

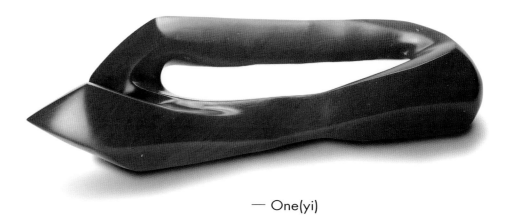

一 One(yi)

2000, 46 X 13 X 13 cm

蕭山石 Stone

仔 Young Animal(zai)

2001, 29 X 20 X 23.5 cm

蕭山石 Stone

弘 Enlarge(hong)

2001, 36.5 X15.5X16 cm

蕭山石 Stone

人 People(ren)

2001, 39.6 X16.3 X13.7cm

蕭山石 Stone

人人-2 Two People-2

2001, 20.5 X17 X20.5 cm
蕭山石 Stone

句 A Sentence(ju)

2001, 44 X 8.5 X22 cm
蕭山石 Stone

鳳 Phonex(fong)

2000, 43 X 27 X28 cm
蕭山石 Stone

眾 The Multitude(jhong)

2000, 40 X 34 X 41 cm
蕭山石 Stone

羽 Feather(yu)

2002, 34 X 12.5 X 18.5 cm

蕭山石 Stone

端 Proper(duan)

2003, 24.5 X14.5 X 29 cm

蕭山石 Stone

飛 Fly(fei)

2003, 33.3 X 17.5 X 20.9cm
蕭山石 Stone

拱 Arch(gong)

2003, 35 X 14 X 19.2 cm
蕭山石 Stone

升-1 Ascend-1, sheng

2003, 24.5 X 15 X·17.5 cm
蕭山石 Stone

舉 Raise(ju)

2003, 38.2 X 31 X 15 cm
蕭山石 Stone

琴 Chinese Harp(qin)

2004, 28.8 X 14.8 X 18 cm
蕭山石 Stone

晴 Sunny(qing)

2004, 26.5 X 21.5 X20.2 cm
蕭山石 Stone

師 Teacher(shi)

2004, 28.3 X 9.2 X 15.5 cm
蕭山石 Stone

掬 Hold in Both Hands(ju)

2004, 29 X 24 X 15 cm
蕭山石 Stone

易 Change(yi)

2005, 23.3 X 10.6 X 12 cm
蕭山石 Stone

申 Explain(shen)

2005, 38.6 X16.7 X15.3 cm
蕭山石 Stone

秋 Autumn(qiu)

2002, 32.5 X 21.5 X 25 cm

蕭山石 Stone

門 Door(men)

2002, 37 X 9.2 X 14.8 cm

蕭山石 Stone

升-2 Ascend-2(sheng)

2005, 24.2 X14.7 X 24.3 cm

蕭山石 Stone

書法
Calligraphy

花 Flower

2008, 53 X 180 cm, ink on paper, 2pcs
宣紙・墨，悉曇文，共2張

悉曇 Siddham

2008, 53 X 180 cm, ink on paper, 2pcs
宣紙・墨，悉曇文，共2張

升 Ascend

2008, 53 X 180 cm, ink on paper, 2pcs
宣紙‧墨，悉曇文，共2張

福 Fortunate

2008, 53 X 180 cm, ink on paper, 2pcs
宣紙‧墨，悉曇文，共2張

娑婆訶 Svaha

2008, 53 X 180 cm, ink on paper
宣紙・墨，悉曇文

禪 Zen (chan)

2008, 53 X 180 cm, ink on paper
宣紙・墨悉，曇文

菩提 Bodhi

2008, 53 X 180 cm, ink on paper
宣紙．墨，悉曇文

美 Beauty

2008, 53 X 180 cm, ink on paper
宣紙．墨，悉曇文

毗沙門天王咒心咒 God of Prosperity Sutra

2008， 53 X 180 cm, ink on paper, 4 pcs
宣紙‧墨，悉曇文，共四張

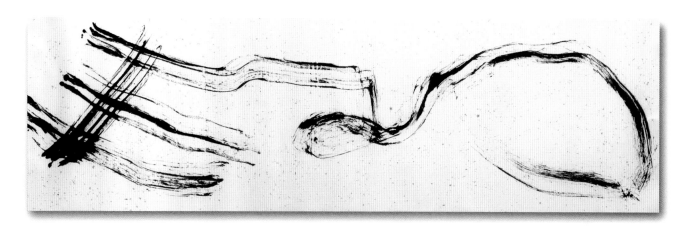

無邊 Borderless

2008, 53 X 180 cm, 2pcs, ink on paper
宣紙‧墨，狂草，共2張

江山清趣 The Delights of Landscape

2008, 53 X 180 cm, ink on paper, 2 pcs
宣紙‧墨，狂草，共2張

青山不語 Silent Green Hills

2008, 53 X 180 cm, ink on paper, 2pcs
宣紙·墨，狂草，共2張

長樂無極 Endless Happiness

2008, 53 X 180 cm, ink on paper, 2pcs
宣紙·墨，狂草，共2張

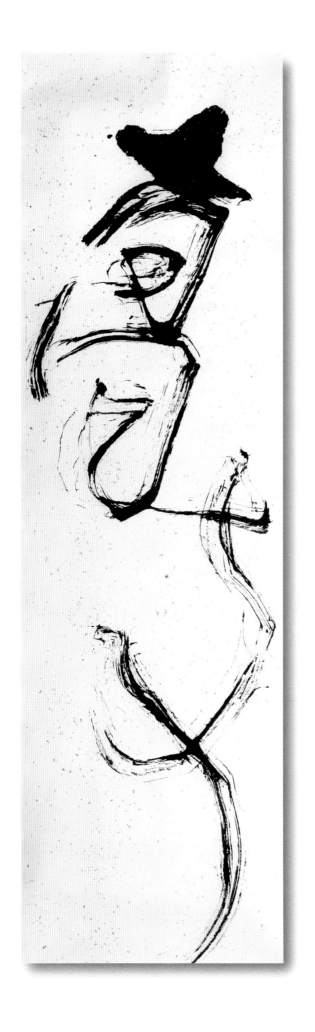
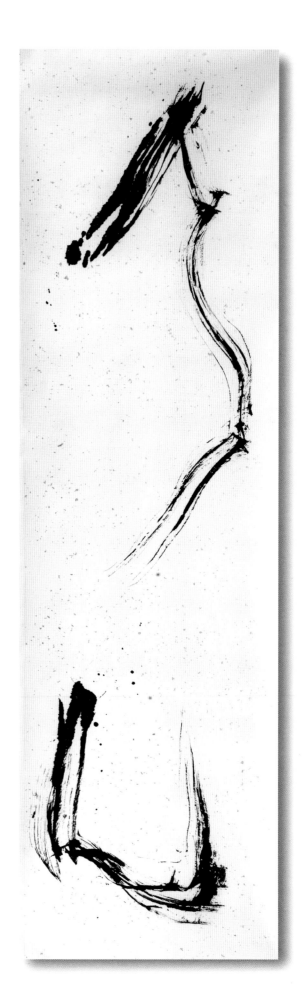

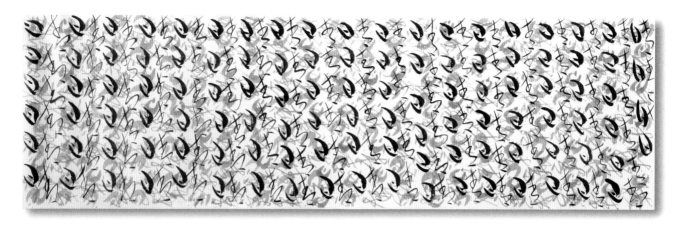

文字皴──晴
Calligraphy-Tsuen: Sunny (qing)

2008, 53 X 180 cm
宣紙・墨 ink on paper

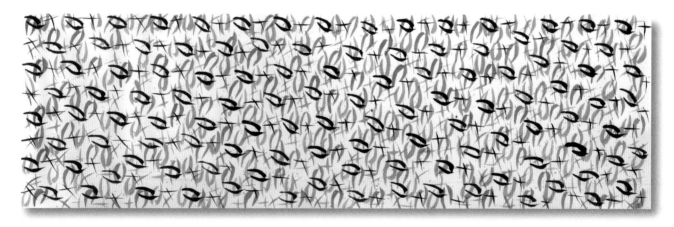

文字皴 Calligraphy-Tsuen
──協 Cooperate (xie)

2008, 53 X 180 cm
宣紙・墨 ink on paper

文字皴 Calligraphy-Tsuen
竹敲風弄菊菊弄風敲竹 p152-156
The Wind Makes Bamboo and Chrysanthemum Tapping

2008, 180 X 53 cm, ink on paper, 10 pcs
宣紙・墨，狂草，共10張

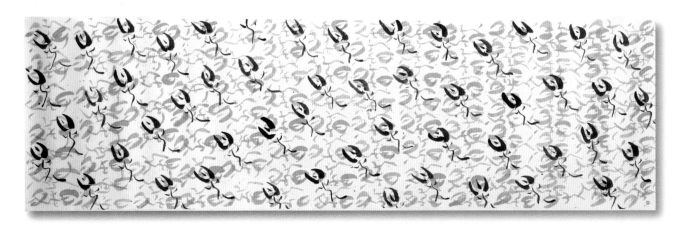

文字皴 Calligraphy-Tsuen
——晃 Calligraphy-Tsuen: Dazzle (huang)

2008, 53 X 180 cm
宣紙・墨 ink on paper

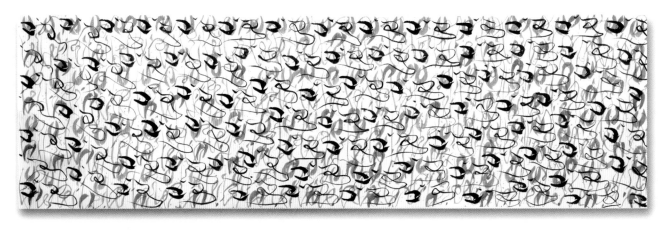

文字皴 Calligraphy-Tsuen
——咏 Calligraphy-Tsuen: Intone (yong)

2008, 53 X 180 cm
宣紙・墨 ink on paper

文字皴 Calligraphy-Tsuen
——口 Mouths

2004, 225 X 140 cm
墨／畫布 ink on canvas

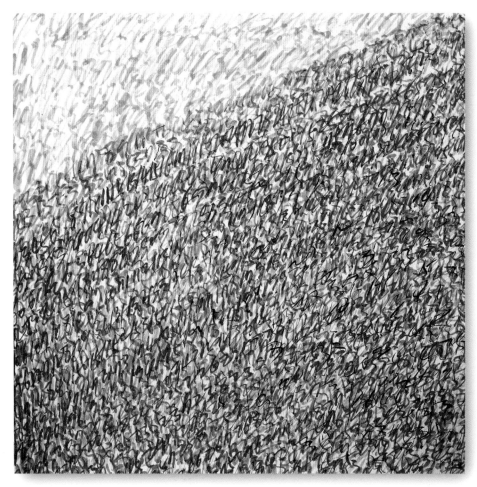

數字皴Number-Tsuen
—— 1, 2, 3...(1)

2005, 69 X 70 cm
墨／宣紙 ink on paper

數字皴Number-Tsuen
—— 1, 2, 3...(2)

2005, 69 X 70 cm
墨／宣紙 ink on paper

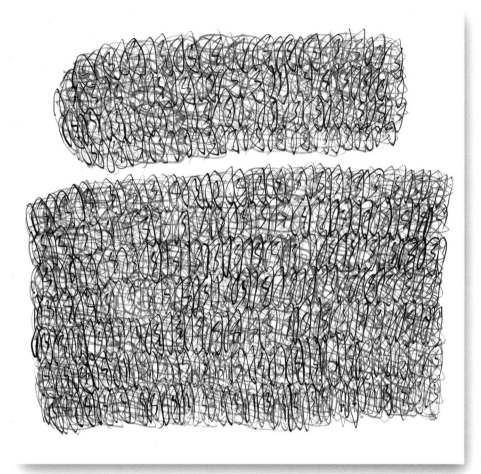

文字皴 Calligraphy-Tsuen
——羽 Feather

2005, 69 X 70 cm
墨／宣紙 ink on paper

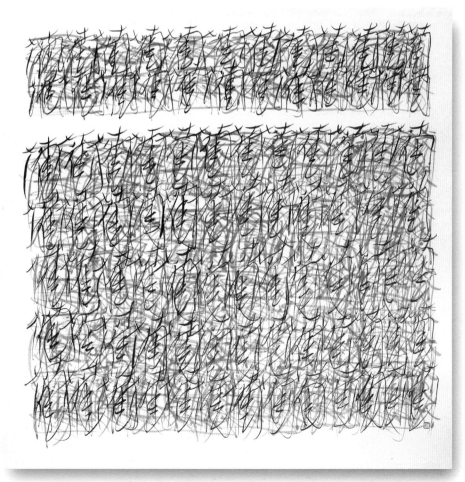

文字皴 Calligraphy-Tsuen
——藺 Rush

2005, 69 X 70 cm
墨／宣紙 ink on paper

書法裝置星垂平野闊月湧大江流
Installation: Stars hang-down level plain vastness,
Moon bobs-from great-river's flow

2008, 68.3 X 425 cm, ink on canvas, 10 pcs
畫布・墨，共10張

Installation: 1620 love you forever

2008,　97 X 162 cm,　canvas · polylon balls · ink · acrylic colors, 3pcs

Siddham is an ancient character of India. Rumor has it that Siddham possesses the mysterious power; therefore, it is regarded as the seed characters called tuo-luo-ni like the charms which represent the mighty power and great prospect of Bodhisattva from the Tibetan Buddhism. Whatever thinking, writing or saying, people can get response from Buddha and Bodhisattva and then are blessed.

The idea of this Work sprang from victims of Szechwan earthquake. Lee-chen-cheng hopes Buddha and Bodhisattva can bless every victim through the power of every seed character. He used 1620 seed characters to make of this work and separated them into 3 groups, per group as 540 seed characters. Every seed character symbolizes the regeneration and the causality. The natural disaster is ruthless but humanity is compassionate. I am you (mandarin pronounced same as"540"). Whatever everything is changed in the world, our hearts are connected forever (the meaning is same that mandarin pronounced as"540"). Pray Buddha and Bodhisattva bless every victim of Szechwan earthquake.

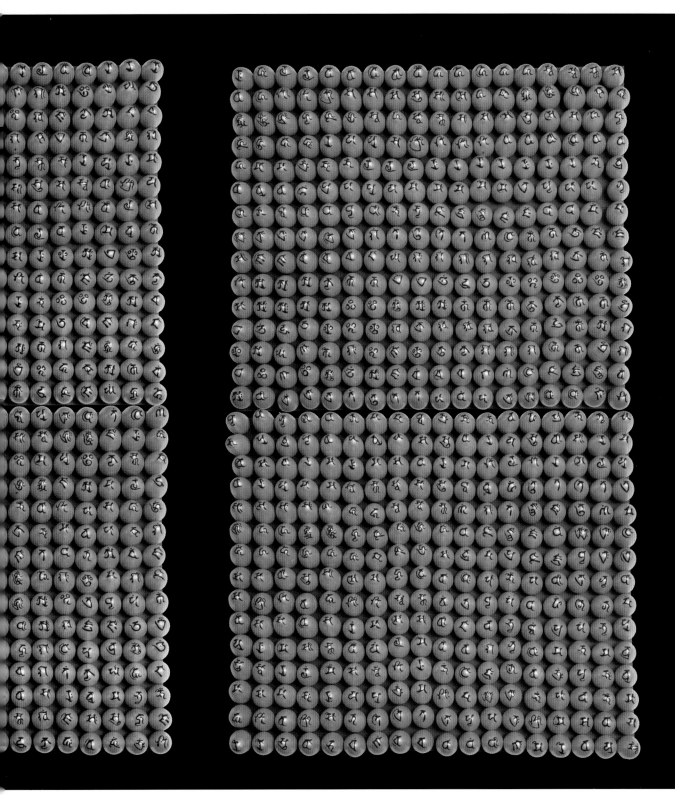

悉曇文裝置——1620一路愛你

2008, 97 X 162 cm，畫布．保麗龍球．墨．壓克力顏料，共3張

悉曇字是印度古老的文字，具有神秘不可思議的力量，密教因而引用爲表徵諸佛菩薩甚深境界與廣大威力的種子字，特稱爲陀羅尼，即眞言咒語。凡觀想、書寫、唸頌者皆能獲得諸佛菩薩殊勝之感應與庇祐，並圓滿一切善願。

本件作品是李鎭成特別爲今年五月間四川震災災民創作的，共用三組1620個種子字組成，每組540字；每一個種子字都象徵一次重生，每顆種子字中既有諸佛菩薩的加持與願力，也有眾生相依相續之因緣。天災固然無情，但人間有情。我中有你、你中有我（540我是你）；無論世界怎麼變，我們的心永遠是相連的（1620一路愛你）。敬願諸佛菩薩福佑四川災民。

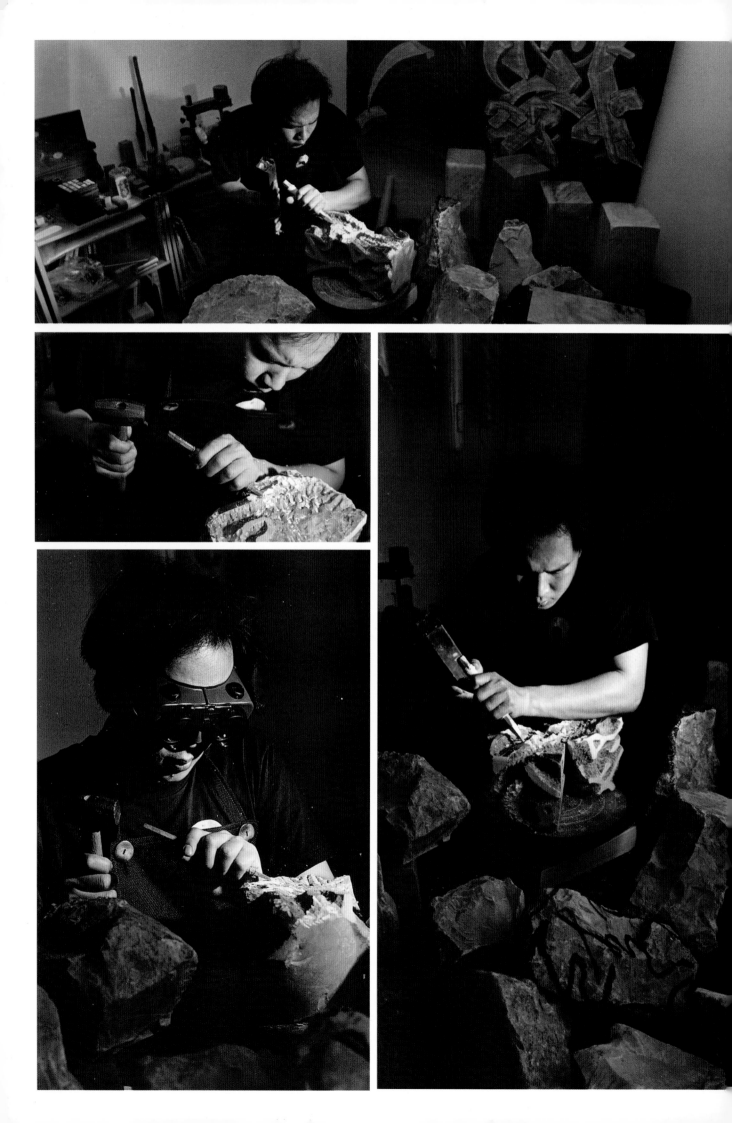

國家圖書館出版品預行編目資料

字在無邊：李鎮成的文字藝術 = Borderless
Calligraphy：Chen-Cheng Lee's series of
script art ／國立歷史博物館編輯委員會
編輯. —— 臺北市：史博館, 2008. 07
　　面；　公分

ISBN 978-986-01-4717-9（平裝）

1.印譜　2.書法　3.作品集

931.7　　　　　　　　　　　97012268

字在無邊

李鎮成的文字藝術

Borderless Calligraphy:
Chen-Cheng Lee's Series of Script Art

發 行 人	黃永川
出 版 者	國立歷史博物館
	台北市100南海路四十九號
	電話：02-23610270
	傳真：02-2-2361-0171
	網站：www.nmh.gov.tw
編　　輯	國立歷史博物館編輯委員會
封面題字	張光賓
主　　編	戈思明
執行編輯	張承宗
展覽顧問	周在台・胡雪紅・李靜芬
展場設計	郭長江・張承宗
攝　　影	陳怡台・柯曉東・蘇益良
文字編輯	李禮君
翻　　譯	張筱玲・羅夢珍・王明燕・鮑依欣
美術設計	羅麗珍
印　　製	日盛印製股份有限公司
定　　價	新台幣800元
出版日期	中華民國九十七年七月
統一編號	1009701723
Ｉ Ｓ Ｂ Ｎ	978-986-01-4717-9
展 售 處	國立歷史博物館文化服務處
	台北市南海路四十九號
	電話：02-23610270

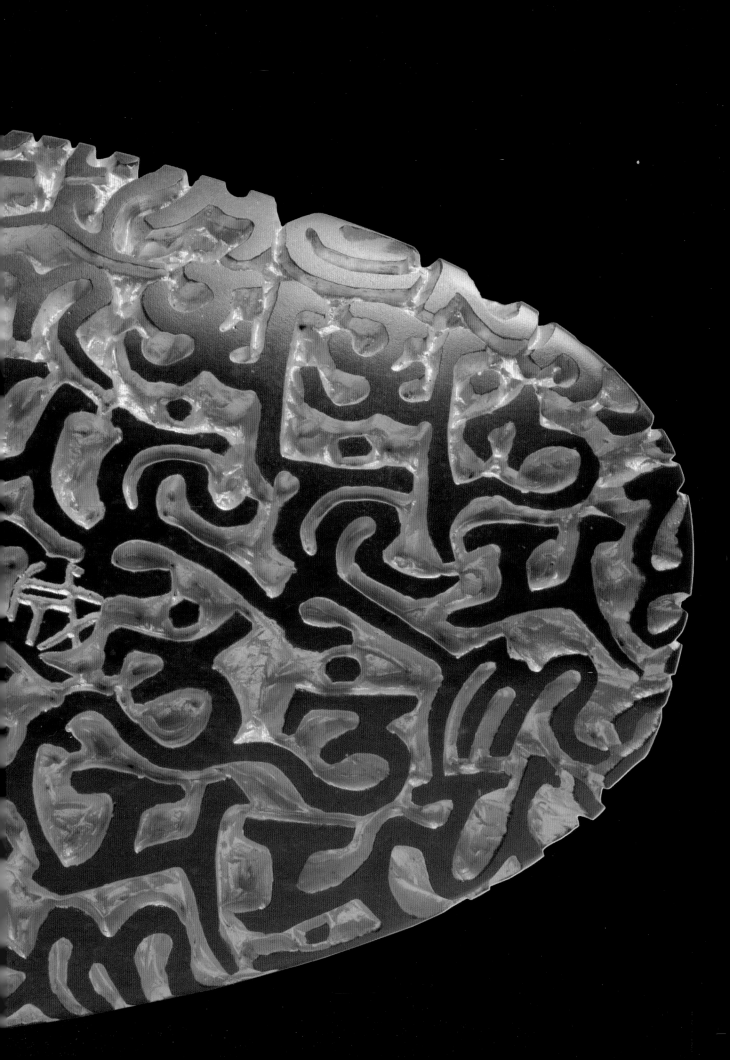